The Case of the
24 MISSING TITLES ...

Over the years many of our American
readers have been distressed that Harlequin
Romances were published in Canada three
months ahead of the United States release
date.

We are pleased to announce that effective
April 1972 Harlequin Romances will have si-
multaneous publication of new titles through-
out North America.

To solve the problem of the 24 MISSING
TITLES (No. 1553 to No. 1576) arrangements will be made with many Harlequin
Romance retailers to have these missing titles
available to you before the end of 1972.

Watch for your retailer's special display!

If, however, you have difficulty obtaining
any of the missing titles, please write us.

Yours truly,

The Publisher
HARLEQUIN ROMANCES.

WELCOME

TO THE WONDERFUL WORLD

of Harlequin Romances!

Interesting, informative and entertaining,
each Harlequin Romance portrays an appealing
love story. Harlequin Romances take you
to faraway places — places with real people
facing real love situations — and
you become part of their story.

As publishers of Harlequin Romances, we're extremely
proud of our books (we've been publishing
them since 1954). We're proud also that Harlequin
Romances are North America's most-read
paperback romances.

Eight new titles are released every month and are
sold at nearly all book-selling stores across
Canada and the United States.

A free catalogue listing all available Harlequin Romances
can be yours by writing to the

HARLEQUIN READER SERVICE,
M.P.O. Box 707, Niagara Falls, N.Y. 14302.
Canadian address: Stratford, Ontario, Canada.

or use order coupon at back of book.

We sincerely hope you enjoy reading
this Harlequin Romance.

Yours truly,

THE PUBLISHERS
    Harlequin Romances

RATA FLOWERS
ARE RED

by

MARY MOORE

HARLEQUIN BOOKS   TORONTO
WINNIPEG

Original hard cover edition published in 1969
by Mills & Boon Limited, 17-19 Foley Street,
London   W1A 1DR, England

© Mary Moore 1969

Harlequin edition published April, 1972

SBN 373-01578-X

The Harlequin trade mark, consisting of the word
HARLEQUIN and the portrayal of a Harlequin, is registered
in the United States Patent Office and in the Canada Trade
Marks Office.

Printed in Canada

CHAPTER I

Judy walked quickly down Oxford Terrace, her heels beating out a rapid tattoo on the pavement. There was really no need to hurry, but the anger inside her had built up a sense of urgency. Now that she had made up her mind to break her engagement, she wanted it finished quickly. She was quite unaware of the admiring glances she drew from the people who were sitting on the seats along the banks of the Avon river, enjoying the warm spring sunshine. She was dressed in a leaf green suit and the sun picked out the copper tints of her shining cap of hair. Her tall-slim figure and long-legged stride seemed to emphasize that spring had really arrived.

Thoughts chased each other chaotically through her mind. How gloriously happy she had been when she left England two months ago to fly to New Zealand. To fly to Bruce. Even the fact that she had finished her nursing training and had passed her Final with honours had been of little significance compared to the fact that she was at last on her way to be with Bruce again after a six-month separation.

Their reunion had been all she had hoped. The parting had, if anything, strengthened their love for each other. His family had

5

welcomed her with open arms. Judy had been delighted. She had expected a certain amount of restraint, perhaps even resentment that Bruce had met and planned to marry an unknown English girl. But Mrs. Clarkson had received her with enthusiasm and had insisted that Judy stay with them until the wedding. Judy had been thrilled at the warmth of her reception and delighted to have the chance to get to know the members of the family intimately. Perhaps that was where she had made the fatal mistake. Perhaps she would have shown more wisdom if she had taken a temporary nursing position while the wedding arrangements were made.

Of course she and Bruce had planned to marry soon after her arrival, but Mrs Clarkson had talked them into waiting for three months to give her time to arrange a proper wedding, as she called it. She had said it would hardly further Bruce's career to have a small, quiet, hole-and-corner wedding. Well, Mrs Clarkson had had her way. But then, thought Judy bitterly, didn't Mrs. Clarkson always get her own way?

Oh, what was the use of going back over the misery and frustration of the last month? She was meeting Bruce now to hand back his ring. It was over. Finished.

The car was parked in the usual place. How often in the last few weeks she had been sitting in the car waiting for Bruce to finish work! It had been one part of the day when she could have him to herself. Her eyes blurred with tears as she blindly groped for the door handle. She got in and slammed the door viciously. She had reached the end of the road. No one could say she hadn't tried to please his mother. At first she had given in because she did not want to start off on the wrong foot. But as time went on Judy discovered that she was always giving in. The only way to satisfy Mrs Clarkson was to surrender completely to her wishes. To do this, Judy had found, was very difficult. Her normal lighthearted, impulsive, independent spirit had been slowly suffocated.

The episode this afternoon had shown her quite clearly that Mrs Clarkson had every intention of managing and controlling their lives after they had married. She made that abundantly clear. This morning Mrs Clarkson had been terribly excited when she had discovered the house next door was up for sale. Judy had thought it was only natural for her to be interested as she would have to live next to the new people. When Mrs Clarkson had rushed off to town to keep an unexpected business appointment, Judy hadn't given it a thought.

Judy felt that she was still numb from the shock of Mrs Clarkson's surprise announcement when she returned home, that she and Bruce had gone to the land agents at lunch time and paid a deposit on the house next door. Judy had sat in horrified silence while Mrs Clarkson had burbled on about how wonderful it would be to have them next door. How she would be able to help Judy with the housekeeping, and when the children came she would be able to advise Judy and teach her how to bring them up. Judy had shivered. Without excusing herself she had gone upstairs and packed her bags. She had rung a taxi and booked a room at Coker's Hotel and left. She had been lucky to leave without Mrs Clarkson's knowledge. She had felt that the least Bruce was entitled to was that she should tell him first that she was breaking her engagement. If she had said goodbye to Mrs. Clarkson she knew that she would not have been able to control herself. She knew also that his mother would have rung Bruce straight away. That woman . . . ! Angrily she pulled off her engagement ring when she heard Bruce approaching the car. She put it on the seat, then turned to stare out the window her side, while she fought desperately to control her emotions.

Judy heard the door open and felt rather than saw Bruce slide into his seat. She noticed his momentary hesitation before he got in, so he must have seen the ring. She must be quick before he started to plead or argue. She continued to gaze out the window. It was easier than facing him and seeing the hurt look on his face.

'I'm giving you back your ring, Bruce. I'm not going to wear it. I am not going to marry you, next month or any other month. We're finished, all washed up. You're not a man, you're a mouse. You're completely spineless, a jellyfish. Your mother has you tied to her apron strings and she'll never let you go. She may be able to direct you, control your every thought, but I'm damned if she's going to boss me!

'What she did this morning was unforgivable. She went down town and without mentioning a word to me, she got you to pay a deposit on that house. What were you thinking of? You could have rung me up and asked what I thought of the idea before you paid over the money. But I can bet it was all your mother's idea to give me a lovely surprise. You gormless nit, she knew I would stop you. She knew, and you did too, that our plan was to buy a new ranch-style home out at New Brighton where we would have young married couples for our neighbours.

'When she told me about it I couldn't believe it. She's a Dracula, a vampire, a—a parasite living on other people's lives!' Judy choked, her eyes were full of tears. 'I've packed my bags and moved to a hotel. I'm leaving Christchurch tomorrow, and I won't tell you where I'm going. I can't—I don't even know myself yet. But I'll get a job

9

somewhere and I'll never see you again, I hope. Oh, Bruce, how could you let her do this to us? I'm ashamed of you. I've begged and pleaded for you to make a stand, but you've got no backbone. Well, haven't you got anything to say?'

'No, nothing really, except that you look quite magnificent when you're in a temper.'

Judy swung round, her startled eyes meeting the amused gaze of a complete stranger.

'Who are you?' she demanded furiously.

'Well, thank God, I'm not that poor jelly-fish Bruce. My name is Mark Palmer. What's yours?'

Ignoring his question, she stuttered, 'W-wh-what are you doing in this car? Get out at once!'

Mark laughed, 'For someone who doesn't like being bossed, you're pretty good at giving orders! And I'm not going to get out. I'm perfectly entitled to be here. This is my car.'

'It is not. It belongs to Bruce Clarkson. I'm his fiancée.'

'From what I heard it doesn't sound like a very permanent position.' The wretched man grinned. 'About the car—I'm afraid you must have been in such a filthy temper that you didn't check very carefully. The car directly behind us is the same colour and make, perhaps that one belongs to Bruce.'

Judy twisted about in her seat and to her

horror realized that the man had spoken the truth. His remark about her temper had not endeared him to her. She had made a complete fool of herself, and the beast looked as if he was enjoying every minute of it. Judy shrugged her shoulders. There was nothing to do but apologize and make as dignified an exit as possible under the circumstances.

' I'm terribly sorry, Mr— Mr—?'

' Mark,' he offered helpfully.

Judy glared at him, ' I'm sorry if I've caused you any inconvenience.' Her voice was coldly polite.

' Oh, don't apologize. I found your performance vastly entertaining. I wouldn't have missed it for worlds. It's not every day I find a long-legged beauty waiting in my car for me. This has really made my day.'

' You're insufferable!' said Judy as she vainly tugged at her short skirt. 'And leave my legs out of the conversation!'

Mark looked in the rear vision mirror. ' Say, would that be your unbeloved Bruce getting into the car now? Poor blighter, he's for it. After practising on me you should be able to give the second performance with even more vim and vigour.'

Judy panicked. She couldn't face Bruce at this moment when she was completely demoralized. It had been bad enough saying all those things when she had been in a white-hot rage, but she simply couldn't do it in cold blood.

'Oh, take me out of here,' she implored Mark. 'Drive around the corner and let me out. Please. I can't face him now.'

'I will if you tell me your name.' Mark offered.

'Judy Somers, as if it matters. Oh, please hurry!'

'Right, Judy, crouch down under the dash-board so that he won't recognize you.' He started the car and pulled out into the traffic. He drove through the Square and down Colombo Street towards the Station until he found a place to park near a well lighted grill-room.

'You can come up for air now,' he told Judy. The only answer he got was a muffled sob. He lit a cigarette and smoked it in silence. When it was finished he spoke to Judy.

'Would you like a loan of my handker-chief?'

'No.'

'You disappoint me. All the best films have the hero offering the damsel in distress a nice clean handkerchief. Sure you won't change your mind?'

He received no reply, but he knew she had stopped crying.

'That chap Bruce must have been a real clot, not to hang on to a girl like you. Fancy letting his mother get in the way. Me, I'd have traded my mother and a couple of aunts as well, to get hold of a girl as pretty as you.'

That brought Judy upright with a jerk. 'You had no right to listen! It was a sneaky thing to do. Why didn't you say something?' Her green eyes flashed fire.

'Here, be fair,' Mark protested. 'I didn't have a chance to get a word in edgeways. Naturally I was surprised to find you here. Before I had time to say a word you blew your top. I took note of your red hair and decided that it was a lot safer to sit out the storm.'

'I have not got red hair!' Judy shouted.

'Well, let's say reddish brown,' said Mark soothingly. Then he spoilt everything by adding, 'And green eyes. Wow, what a combination!'

'I have brown hair and hazel eyes.' Judy glared at him, then looked around her. 'Where are we?'

'In Colombo Street, down near the Station.'

'Good, I know how to find my way to the hotel from here.'

'I'll drive you wherever you want to go. Which hotel are you staying at?'

'Coker's. But there's no need to drive me there. It's just along here. I can walk,' and then she added belatedly, 'Thanks.'

'Would you like a cigarette?' Mark suggested.

13

'No, thanks, Mr— er Mr—?'

'Mark. Really, Judy, after all we've been through together you can hardly insist on formality,' he laughed.

Suddenly the humour of the situation struck her. It was quite crazy. Like a Mad Hatter's tea party. Judy's lips trembled, a dimple quirked and then she smiled. She looked at Mark and then they both broke into peals of laughter.

Oh, the blessed healing relief of shared laughter! Judy felt that she had shed a strait-jacket she'd worn for weeks. Slowly she sobered up.

'I really am most awfully sorry to have been such a nuisance to you, M-Mark,' she said shyly. 'This has been a terrible day for me, as you may have guessed. Then I had to make matters worse by climbing into the wrong car and breaking my engagement with the wrong man. I think you took my whole performance remarkably well.' She gave him her normal wide smile. It was amazing how much at ease she felt with him. She should have felt small and humiliated, but there was something about him that gave her confidence.

'Why, thank you, ma'am, for them kind words. I gather you've had a fairly grim time lately. Now to show that I really am forgiven, will you come and have a bite with me?'

'No, thank you,' replied Judy quickly.

'I've got a lot to do.'

'I'll say you have,' said Mark blandly. 'You've got to see Bruce and break off your engagement. That won't be easy. He'll have probably traced you to the hotel by now and be waiting for you. I think you'd be better able to face the difficulties if you had a good meal first. What do you say?'

Judy still hesitated. He was probably right about Bruce. By now they would have discovered her missing. It was an easy task to ring around the hotels to see if she had registered. She needed more time.

'Another thing,' Mark grinned at her. 'Just a small point, of course, but the next show is going to lack fire if you haven't got your ring to throw back at him. I'll keep it safely for you until we've had something to eat.'

Judy was appalled. She had completely forgotten about the ring. Wouldn't she have felt terrible if she had jumped out of the car earlier and left the ring with Mark? How would she have traced him? How would she have explained to Bruce?

'Goodness me, you wouldn't resort to blackmail to get your own way? Or would you?'

'I wouldn't hesitate. I'm a desperate character. I would even consider kidnapping if all else failed.'

'Then it looks as if I have no option. I'm only a poor defenceless female, entirely at your mercy. I will accept your gracious invitation.'

'That's my girl! But I'm not sure about the defenceless female bit. Sorry I can't take you to dinner, but I haven't much time. I have to get on the road home. I have a two-hundred-mile drive in front of me tonight, so let's nip into this grill-room and see what they have to offer.'

He walked round and opened the door for her. Taking her arm, he led her into the pleasant warmth of the grill-room. She was surprised to find that she only came up to his shoulder. She was quite tall herself, so he must be about six feet or a bit over. Idly she wondered what he did for a living. She guessed he would be a professional man, or perhaps an up-and-coming business executive.

They found a table and gave their order, Mark leaned forward and regarded her speculatively. 'Pardon me for referring to the earlier part of our meeting, but it's of great importance to me—at least one thing you said is. You said that you were going to leave Christchurch and also that you were going to have to find a job. Did you mean that, or were you just saying it to bring Bruce to heel?'

'I meant every word I said.'

'What sort of work did you have in mind?'

'I'm a trained nurse. I don't suppose it

16

would be hard to get a position. I would like to go to some small country district, if possible.'

'It's fate, that's what it is! But I'd better start at the beginning. I'm a farmer. What are you looking so startled for?'

'You don't look like a farmer,' Judy stated positively.

Mark shook his head sadly. 'You townies are all the same. Just because a fellow doesn't wear gumboots and chew straw all the time, he doesn't look like a farmer! For your information, I don't wear this suit when I'm milking the cows. Okay, where was I? Oh yes. I have a farm on the West Coast.'

'What sort of farm? How big is it?'

'Eight hundred acres. It's a mixed farm. Mainly devoted to town supply milking, but I do have a few hundred ewes and have a few run cattle. I came over today to give a paper at Lincoln College.'

'What was the subject of the paper?' interrupted Judy.

'Budgeting. How to increase production with only limited capital.'

'I thought all New Zealand farmers were rich.'

'A few of them are very rich, a lot of them are comfortably off, but the majority of them are like me, scratching for a living. Farming on a shoestring and hoping they don't slip and hang themselves with it. Now don't interrupt. I lose the thread of my discourse. I have a pair of ten-year-old twins at home, and until six weeks ago my mother stayed to look after them. She has had a lot of worry which I won't go into just now, but the result was that she suffered a slight heart attack. She has been in hospital ever since.

'The doctor said that if I could get some-one to help, I could bring her home. She doesn't need nursing, only someone to keep an eye on her, and see that she doesn't overdo things for a start. I had one housekeeper a couple of weeks ago, but she turned out to be an alcoholic. I came in one afternoon to dis-cover her rolling drunk with the twins as interested spectators, so she had to go. This is the busiest time of the year on the farm. I simply can't stay in with the kids when they come home from school, and although they're out with me a lot, I can't take them with me in all weathers.

'I put an ad in the Press saying I would be in Christchurch today and would interview any applicants for the job. Two applied and both were hopeless.'

'In what way were they hopeless?' asked Judy.

Mark waited until the waiter had served their meal and left. He looked slightly em-barrassed. 'One of them wanted an astro-nomical wage, which I can't afford. The other one intimated that she was quite prepared to offer me all the home comforts, and I mean all. She said quite frankly that she would be quite happy to accommodate me if I didn't like sleeping alone.' He shuddered.

'I don't believe you!' Judy's gay laugh rang out.

'It wasn't funny,' Mark glowered. 'After that I tried all the employment agencies and the Labour Exchange. Nothing. No one wants to go out in the country. Now, I know I've got a colossal nerve, but I have to ask. Would you be interested in a position like that? You did say you preferred the country. I don't want to pressure you, but even if you could come for two or three weeks it would be wonderful. What do you say?'

Judy gave him a long steady look. Of course she knew that she could not judge a man's character at one glance, but his clean-cut features made a favourable first impression. He had a strong deeply tanned face, a firm mouth and determined chin. There were laughter lines around his eyes—blue eyes that held a glimmer of amusement.

'I won't press you for an answer. Eat up, or your meal will go cold. I don't expect you to take me at face value, you know. I'll give you the names of several folk here in Christ-church who will vouch for my character. This steak is really good. I was starving!'

As Judy ate her steak, eggs and chips she was surprised to find how hungry she was.

She had been so much on edge lately that she had not felt like eating much. She must be mad to think of going off with a man she hardly knew. But it was a job. And what was the alternative? Leaving Christchurch tomorrow for an unknown destination and then applying for a position. She was seriously tempted. After all, he did offer references, and there was his mother and children there. And he did have a sense of humour, that was most important.

'How do you know I'll be suitable?' she asked curiously. 'I haven't any references, and I hardly think Mrs Clarkson would give me one.'

'You'll be just right. You're strong and healthy, and you'll need to be to keep up with the twins. You can laugh at yourself: this I consider a most necessary virtue. You've shown that you have a fine independent spirit. You'll fit in just perfectly.'

'You don't even know if I can cook,' Judy protested.

Mark laughed, 'Even if you can't boil water, I would still want you. To have someone as pretty as you about the place would make everyone feel so good, it wouldn't matter what we ate.'

'Flattery will get you nowhere,' Judy told him firmly. She couldn't help feeling pleased all the same. Mark had shown quite obviously that he liked and admired her. After weeks of trying to walk a narrow tightrope of behaviour to gain Mrs Clarkson's approval, she suddenly felt free.

'Tell me about your children. What are their names?'

'They aren't my children,' Mark looked horrified, 'they're my brother's kids. You must have misunderstood me. Peter and Vicki are living with me while their parents are overseas. I'm not married.'

Not married, thought Judy, and was ashamed of the thrill of pleasure she felt.

Mark took a piece of paper from his pocket, and a pen, and wrote down three addresses. 'Here are the names and addresses and phone numbers of three people who will speak for me. The first one is Basil Watson, of Watson, Watson and Taylor, solicitors. I was at school with him. The next one is the Vicar of All Saints Church. And the last is my aunt, Mrs Morris. She's rather a pet. Go out and see her. She would come and help me herself, only her husband is an invalid. Well, what's the verdict?'

'I'll come.' Judy's face lit up with delight as she imagined what Mrs Clarkson's reaction to her impulsive decision would be. Her slightly slanted witch-green eyes sparkled wickedly. 'I've decided the devil you know is better than the devil you don't know.'

Mark pretended to be hurt. 'I don't care for your reasoning, my dear girl. I find your

allusion of my character extremely painful.'
Then he smiled, 'But I'm very relieved that
you've decided to take us on. You've taken
a tremendous load off my shoulders. You're
definitely not the mercenary type. You
haven't even asked what I'm going to pay
you.' He named a figure far in excess of what
Judy expected.

'Certainly not. I wouldn't get near as
much as that at the hospital. I think ten
pounds a week—sorry, I mean twenty dollars
—would be generous. It's hard to get used to
thinking in dollars and cents. And I'll come
for a fortnight's trial. If I don't like it, or if
you don't find me suitable, we can stop there
with no hard feelings. Agreed?'

'I think a fortnight's trial is a good idea,
but I'm not having you working for a pit-
tance. I'm not a pauper. Say I pay you the
same wage you would get from the hospital.
Will that suit you?'

'Yes,' agreed Judy thankfully. 'When do
I start?'

'I'd like to take you with me tonight, but
I can hardly expect you to set off into the
night with a complete stranger. There's a
railcar which leaves Christchurch at ten-
twenty every day. Give me that envelope and
I'll write my address and phone number on
it. You can check up on me tomorrow and if
you haven't changed your mind, send me a
telegram saying which day you're travelling.

You buy a ticket to Stillwater and I'll meet you there. The railcar gets in about two thirty, I think.'

Mark sat back and lit a cigarette. 'Well, that's all the details taken care of. I'll run you back to the hotel and get on my way.' He picked up the tab, then took her ring from his pocket and put it in front of her. 'That young chap of yours must be very unimaginative. Fancy choosing an ordinary diamond ring for a girl like you. If I bought you an engagement ring it would be a large square emerald.'

'It's a very valuable ring,' Judy's eyes flashed. 'And you never will have to worry about buying me an engagement ring. If I ever get married, and I don't think I will, I'll take good care to choose an orphan. There'll be no mother messing up my wedding plans another time!'

'But you haven't met my mother yet. She's really something. Plenty of girls have wanted to marry me just to get her for their mother-in-law.'

Judy giggled, her anger forgotten. He really was ridiculous! She placed the ring in her purse and went out to the car.

Mark drove the short distance to the hotel, and parked the car. He turned to Judy, his voice serious for once. 'Judy, just a minute before you get out. I have something to say to you. You're only a young girl, and your family are a long way away. You're making a big decision when you hand back that ring. Take my advice, don't be hasty. This afternoon you were very upset. Perhaps you said things you didn't really mean. You've had time to cool down. Think carefully before you act. I suggest that you ring his home to let them know where you are, then tell him you'll see him in the morning. I think it's always best to have a good sleep before deciding anything important. You know the old adage " sleep on it " '

'No, I wouldn't sleep. This decision isn't as sudden as you think. I've been worried for the last month. I've given it plenty of serious thought. I won't change my mind,' Judy said stubbornly.

' Bruce is still in love with you, I presume?' Mark made it a question.

' Yes.'

'And you must have loved him or you wouldn't have promised to marry him. Don't you love him now?'

'Yes—no. Oh, don't keep at me! I don't know what I feel for him. I did love him very much when we met in England, but he seems a different person in his own country. I still like him, but I feel sorry for him now. He's clever and intelligent, and is highly respected in the firm where he works. It's just his private life that's such a mess. He never makes a move without his mother's approval. I thought if he would transfer to another town our marriage would have a chance. I nearly had him persuaded, but he talked it over with his mother, and she became so upset that he dropped the whole idea.' Judy's voice was bitter.

'Perhaps you over-estimate his mother's control. Once you're his wife you will have a lot more influence with him.'

'Not if she's living next door. Anyway, whose side are you on?' Judy cried accusingly.

'I'm not on either side. Personally, I hope you get rid of him and come over to the Coast, but I don't want you to make any mistakes that you may be sorry for afterwards.'

'I'm sorry,' muttered Judy contritely. 'I know I'm a bit touchy on this subject. And it's good of you to bother with me, especially when you have a long drive in front of you. But I'm not a child. I'm twenty-three, old enough to know my own mind. I know now that I couldn't marry Bruce, I couldn't be happy with a man I didn't respect.'

'Mrs Clarkson says she only wants the best for us, and I'm sure that's the truth. She refers to her interference as, quote, "a gentle guiding hand," unquote. I know that she had many good points, she is an excellent housekeeper, a marvellous cook, better than I will ever be. She's on all sorts of committees, and works hard. She has the best garden in the street. Perhaps she does always know best, but I want to be free to make my own mistakes. Oh, you don't want to hear all this.'

Mark encouraged her, ' Tell me. I'm interested, and it may help you if you get it off your chest.'

Judy continued, ' You would think being so busy, she would be happy to let us go our own way, but no, she takes an interest in every move we make. For instance, Bruce and I planned to have a small quiet wedding shortly after I arrived. His mother said it wouldn't help his career to have a rushed hole-and-corner wedding. She said it would take her three months to prepare for the type of wedding she wished us to have. So we waited. I wanted to have Bruce's two little nieces as my attendants, but she thought it more fitting to have three girls of my own age. I gave in. Honestly I don't want to bore you with all these petty details, but you must understand that there's no satisfying Mrs Clarkson. No arrangement is too small to escape her notice. If Bruce and I plan to dine out, she says she has people coming for dinner especially to meet me. So we stay in. When we discuss buying furniture, whatever I choose, she has some good reason why it's not suitable, and every time she talks Bruce around to her way of thinking. He's like putty in her hands. I could go on and on, but I won't. This afternoon when she told me we were going to live next door, I could see the writing on the wall. I've got to get out and quickly.'

'I'm sorry you've had such a rough time, Judy,' Mark said sympathetically. 'Bruce sounds to me as if he's sadly lacking in intestinal fortitude. He deserves to lose you. And as for his mother, she sounds a real beaut.' He got out of the car and went round to open the door for Judy, then escorted her to the hotel.

Taking her cold hand in his large warm one, he said goodbye. 'I'm glad we met, Judy. Remember if you change your mind, you have my best wishes. If you decide to come over to the Coast we'll do our best to see you enjoy yourself. Send a wire and I'll be waiting for you.' He gave her hand a comforting squeeze and walked away to his car.

CHAPTER II

Judy caught the railcar with only minutes to spare. Her face was flushed as she sank thankfully into her seat. What a rush! She felt quite jubilant. Last night, when Mark had driven off, she had promised herself that she would be on the railcar the next morning come what may. And here she was. She did not know why the thought of catching the railcar had become so important, but she had used it as a crutch to support her through the painful meeting with Bruce last night.

He had been waiting for her when she returned to the hotel. He had been worried and upset about her disappearance. Poor Bruce, she had felt a swift rush of pity as she saw his anxious face.

They had gone for a drive. The name of the place she did not remember, but it had been a beautiful spot. The sky had been alive with brilliant stars and the light of the full moon shone on the sea. The sound of the waves crashing on the shore had seemed but an echo of her own smashed hopes and dreams.

There she had told Bruce she would not marry him. He had been quite marvellous, she had to admit that. He had listened to what she had to say, without interrupting or arguing. Bruce had agreed that his mother was too possessive and that he had been unfair to Judy. He had been quiet and controlled, but had not attempted to hide how deeply hurt he was. He begged for another chance.

Judy had found herself weakening. She had loved him very much, but she knew deep in her heart that their marriage would not work out. She was sorry for him, but pity was no foundation on which to base a happy marriage.

Bruce had promised to see the land agent first thing in the morning and cancel the deal even if it cost him money. He promised to apply for a transfer to Wellington and he was reasonably certain it could be arranged within two months. He promised to agree to anything Judy wanted, if only she would marry him. He had been quietly determined and sure of himself, adamant that he would not accept her decision as final. Judy had never admired him more. If only he had shown that firmness with his mother a month ago there would have been no broken engagement now. Even so Judy had held to her purpose. She was scared to trust him. She had been hurt too often. The magic had gone from their romance.

Finally he realized that she was determined to give his ring back. 'Very well, Judy, I'll take the ring and keep it in the hope that one day you'll let me put it back on your finger where it belongs. I love you so much. I know that I've been a fool. If you give me another chance I'll make amends. Perhaps it's a good idea for you to go away, but you must let me know where you will be. Let me write to you.' His voice was desperate. 'Let me see you once again. Take all the time you want to reconsider your decision. One month, two months, I don't care how long, but you've got to let me see you once more.'

Judy had not the heart to refuse to see him again, although she told him it would be useless. She would not change her mind. She advised him to get away from his mother and start living his own life, not for her sake, but for his own.

They had parted friends, but Judy knew that they had lost something very precious. It would never be the same between them. She had gone to bed shaken and miserable, and had cried herself to sleep.

The clickety-clack of the wheels and the rocking motion of the railcar were soothing. Her thoughts turned to what lay ahead. She began to feel a bit apprehensive. Perhaps she had been too impulsive jumping at the first offer of a job.

What did she know about Mark Palmer? Nothing. This morning she had decided that since Mark had given her the position on face value, it would be mean of her to check up on his credentials. Now she was not so sure. She might be heading into a very difficult situation. Then and only then did she remember that she had not sent the telegram to say she would be arriving today. What an idiot she was!

'Good morning. Mind if I sit here?'

Judy looked up startled to find an elderly man putting his case in the luggage rack above her head. She smiled and moved over nearer the window.

The man sat down and gave Judy a friendly smile. 'Cass Davis is the name. My daughter doesn't approve of me smoking and so she booked me into a non-smoking compartment. I've just got the guard to change me through here.' He lit a cigarette with obvious satisfaction and winked at her. 'What the eye doesn't see the heart doesn't grieve over!'

Judy had to laugh.

Mr Davis settled down to read his paper, and Judy stared blankly out of the window. Her mind filled with unhappy thoughts. She would have to send a cable to her parents to let them know the wedding was off. Not that the news would affect them much. They had let Judy go her own way for a long time. She had been twelve when they had been divorced. They had been pleased that Judy had accepted the breaking up of their home with apparent indifference. But that indifference had only been on the surface. The hurt had gone deep, and the feeling of insecurity had taken years to conquer. She had been sent to boarding school and had spent the vacations being shared equally between them. They had both remarried and had young families. Judy knew they still loved her, but the feeling of being a visitor persisted whenever she visited either household.

From this experience she had become determined to make sure that if she ever married it would be for life. She would not be guilty of giving any child of hers that lost lonely feeling that she had suffered when her parents split up. But how could you be sure that love would last? She had believed that Bruce was the right man for her. She was shaken with doubts. She had read somewhere that children from broken homes had less chance of making a successful marriage than those from happy, secure homes. Well, if that was the case she would never marry.

' Have you ever been to the Coast before?'

Judy suddenly realized that her seat companion was speaking to her.

' No, this is my first visit,' she replied, only too happy to have someone to talk to. Anything was better than sitting brooding.

' Great place. I've just been on a visit to my daughter in Christchurch and I'm real glad to be heading home. My son has a farm in Totara Flat, and I live with him and his family. His wife is a great girl. I potter about the place and do odd jobs for them. I'm real lucky I have such a good home. You know, I went out to an old people's home when I was in Christchurch, to see a friend of mine. It would fair break your heart to see those old folk. I reckon it would be a living death to be shut in one of those places. Mind you, I'm not saying they're not well cared for, but after a life of hard work, to be shoved in there by your kids as if you were a nuisance! It must be hell.'

'It doesn't sound as if you have to worry, Mr Davis,' Judy consoled him.

'No, I'm one of the lucky ones. I went over to live with June, she's my daughter in Christchurch, when Mother died. She made me real welcome, you know, but I couldn't take city life. Not after living on the Coast all my life. Where are you from? You're not a New Zealander, I can tell by your accent.'

'I'm English. I've been in New Zealand nearly two months. If you've lived on the West Coast all your life you must know a great deal about it.'

'Wonderful people on the Coast. They're different to the rest of the New Zealanders, I reckon, more open, more friendly, more hospitable. They're not very partial to law and order. I don't mean they're lawless, just a bit touchy about too many rules and regulations. They obey the laws they find reasonable.

The others they just ignore. They're basically very honest people, so there's very little crime over there. No, it's just the petty little laws they get into bother with, like the one about closing pubs at six. It never worked on the Coast. Damn silly law anyway. I could tell you some real funny things about the Coast if I had a mind to.'

'Oh, do tell me,' Judy encouraged eagerly.

That was all Cass Davis needed. For an hour he talked and Judy listened, entranced. He told her of people and places up and down the Coast—stories about the early pioneers and the hardships they faced. Some of the tales were sad, stark tragedy, and others were hilariously funny. It soon became clear to Judy that this man knew and loved the open, outdoor life, that he loved the bush, the mountains and the birds, and even the wild treacherous rivers. No wonder he couldn't settle down to city life. He talked interestingly and well.

'Mustn't bore you too much, miss,' he said eventually, ' but now you've got some idea of what makes a West-Coaster. Other people call them rugged, individualists, but they're good-hearted folk and I know you'll be glad you came. I'm going to have a bit of a snooze now. Wake me up when we get to Otira for lunch.'

After listening to the old man Judy found herself looking at the bush and mountains with different eyes. The scenery was magnificent. The railcar was now travelling an hour late because of the washouts after the flood last week.

They stopped at Otira, and when Mr Davis returned he had two friends with him. He introduced them to Judy as Sam and Bill Grey. They tipped the next seat over so they could sit facing Judy and Mr Davis.

The short fat jolly-looking one, named Sam, laughed as he sat down, 'Trust old Casanova Davis to choose a seat beside the prettiest girl on the railcar!'

Judy had to smile when she heard the nickname. She guessed it had been well earned. Anyone as handsome and charming as he was at seventy must have been a great man with the ladies in his youth. She enjoyed listening to their conversation, but when she heard Mark Palmer's name mentioned she really became interested. The two men were farmers and had been at Lincoln College when Mark had given his paper.

'Clever young feller,' Sam Grey said. 'Tough too. When he first took on that farm none of us thought he'd make a go of it, but he sure is holding his own.'

'Don't think I know him at all,' admitted Cass. 'He's not the Palmer that plays full-back for the Coast team, is he?'

'Yeah, that's him. Plays a good game, too. He was picked for the Island trials, but he told the Rugby Union he wasn't available. Pity too, I reckon he had a fair chance of making the All Blacks. Great boot on him, and he's not scared to tackle.'

Judy was really alert and listening intently.

Bill Grey laughed, ' He looks such an easy-going chap, but you don't want to be fooled by that smile of his. No, sir. He can look after himself—remember that time he gave those Walters boys a thrashing? They thoroughly deserved it. Remember that, Sam?'

' Yeah, I won't forget that in a hurry,' Sam chuckled. ' It was like this, Cass. The boy inherited the farm from his uncle. Before he had time to get to know his own cattle there was a sale at Ngahere. Old Walters had a mob in, and the boy sat up on the rail watching them being sold. He didn't realize that half them were his own cattle.' The men all laughed.

Judy was horrified, before she could stop herself she burst out, ' Why didn't someone tell him?'

'Listen, miss, if he was too silly to know his own cattle he deserved to lose them. I didn't know they weren't old Walters' cattle, and even if I had known, I wouldn't have poked my nose into something that didn't concern me. Get yourself into a lot of bother that way. Anyway, when young Palmer mustered his cattle he found out he was short and went looking for them. Someone must have told

36

him what was what, so he kept his eyes open. A couple of months later he missed about forty ewes. He trailed them up the riverbed and could see that they'd been driven. He found them inside Walters' boundary fence. He opened the gate to drive them back when the two Walters boys came on the scene and there was hell to pay.'

Bill chipped in, 'It must have been a beaut fight. I called in to see Palmer that night and he was a real mess. He was smiling even though it must have hurt him. He said that the other two looked worse than he did and he bet me it would be a long time before they pinched any more stock from him.'

Judy was disgusted. 'What an uncivilized way to behave!'

'Uncivilized it might be, young lady,' Bill said, 'but sometimes it's the only way a man can make his point. Those two boys were spoiling for a fight and they got more than they bargained for. What did you expect Palmer to do? Walk away and leave his sheep?'

Judy protested, 'Surely you have a police force? He could have gone home and called them.'

'You don't know what you're talking about, if you'll pardon me for saying so. If he'd left the sheep he would have never seen them again. By the time the police got into action they would have been miles away.

37

The police are willing to help, but cases like that are well-nigh impossible to prove.'

Judy protested, 'What about earmarks and brands? Don't they prove who owns the sheep?'

'Up to a point they're satisfactory. Well, farmers aren't allowed to use branding fluid any more, as a means of identification, because it spoils the wool,' Cass pointed out. 'And earmarks are chancy. Anyone can go to Addington sale and buy sheep with his neighbour's earmark on. There are sheep there from three or four different provinces and earmarks can't help being duplicated. A dishonest man has plenty of ways of covering his tracks, believe me. The police move too slow. By the time you notify them and they come out to investigate, the stolen stuff is hanging up in a butcher's yard, nine times out of ten. No, the boy did the only thing he could.'

'You all seem to accept it so calmly. Is there much stock stolen?'

''Course there is. Anyone who has sheep expects to lose a few lambs over the Christmas period. Fellers come out from town and nip off one for their dinner. Nobody really minds, even if you did you've got a fat chance of stopping them,' Bill explained. 'No, the real trouble starts if you get a crook for a neighbour. Most farmers are honest enough, but occasionally you get one like old Walters in the district, then you've got to watch him like a hawk. Cunning old devil, he is. I'm glad he's not a neighbour of mine.'

'You bet,' agreed Sam, 'and Palmer has enough on his plate without any extra. Do you remember old Jack Palmer, Cass?'

'Yes, I met him once or twice. Seemed a nice bloke.'

'Well, Mark is his nephew. Jack died four years ago and the boy got the farm with a few strings attached. Rumour has it that he and the old boy didn't see eye to eye. Mark went to Lincoln College and came back with a lot of high-falutin' ideas. They used to argue like mad. Mark became a farm advisory officer after he got his degree. The story is that Jack left the farm to Mark in his will provided he can double the production in five years. He made him pay a pretty steep lease for it during those five years too, so the boy hasn't much money to prove his fancy theories. But I'll say this for him, he works like a man possessed. We all thought he wouldn't have a hope, but we could be wrong, I reckon.'

Bill said, 'Poor beggar, he lost a lot of stock in a big flood the first year he was there. Knocked him for a six, it did, but it didn't knock that smile off his face. I like him. He's a decent chap. Never too busy to give a neighbour a helping hand. He was coming past my place one day just as my trailer broke and five wool bales came off on the ground. First time I met him really. He came straight in and gave me a hand to get them on the truck. They were heavy brutes of things to lift, but it didn't seem to bother him at all. I hope he makes the grade.'

The railcar had stopped again. It was going to be quite late by the time they reached Stillwater. The men were talking about someone Judy didn't know, so she sat quiet and thoughtful. There was more to Mark Palmer than she had first thought. It was hard to reconcile the pleasant, debonair young man she had met last night with the determined fighter these men had talked about.

She felt rather embarrassed that she had not mentioned that she was going to stay at his farm—almost as if she had been eavesdropping on a conversation. However, there really had not been an opening to say anything, and now the subject had changed. What had that man said? Something about not being fooled by his smile. Judy thought ruefully that the warning had come a bit late for her.

CHAPTER III

On arrival at the Stillwater Station, Judy collected her cases and put them in the waiting room where there was a lovely big coal fire burning. She found a public telephone box and tried the number Mark had given her. There was no answer. She went to the cafeteria and ordered a cup of tea. It was steaming hot and she felt much more cheerful when she had finished it. Once again she tried the telephone, and this time a little girl's voice answered her.

'Could I speak to Mark Palmer, please?' Judy asked.

'Uncle Mark is still at the shed. I'm Vicki. Can I take a message?'

'Hullo, Vicki. Could you tell me when your uncle will be home?'

'I don't know. He's nearly finished.'

'Would you tell him that Judy Somers is at Stillwater Station, and ask him to come and get me, please.'

'Who?'

'Judy Somers. He'll know who I am. You won't forget, will you?'

'No. Goodbye.' Judy heard the receiver click down. She felt annoyed with herself as she returned to the waiting room. If she had remembered to send the telegram she wouldn't have to sit here waiting. She was very tired after her sleepless night last night and the long railcar journey. Time passed so slowly, and her head began to nod.

She woke with a start. How long had she been asleep? She looked at her watch. It was six o'clock. Surely Mark must have finished his work now? It was dark outside. Perhaps the little girl had forgotten to give him the message. More frightening still was the thought that maybe he did not want her. He would not just leave her here. Or would he?

Then she saw his tall rangy figure come through the door. He walked over to her and bent and kissed her quickly on the cheek. 'These your cases? Right, come on, follow me. I'm late.'

Judy was furious, but he had disappeared through the doorway before she had time to recover. She grabbed her bag and small case and hurried after him. She followed him down the platform and across the railway lines to his car. He had put her cases in by the time she got there and was holding the door open for her.

'What do you mean by kissing me? You've got a nerve! I've a good mind not to go with you.'

'Oh, come on, now. Hop in. The kids are waiting. Imagine how my shares have shot up with the locals after them seeing me kiss such a pretty girl. Now jump in and stop making a fuss. I'm in a hurry.'

Judy got in. Put his shares up, had she? Well, if he ever tried that again, she would give the locals something to talk about! She waited for him to get in and drive off before she really gave him a piece of her mind, but he didn't give her a chance.

'Wonderful to have you here, Judy. You don't know how wonderful. I really didn't think you would come. Now, I've got to go in here for a minute and see a chap. I won't take you as we must get back to the kids before they murder each other.'

He was back very quickly and drove rapidly back down the road they had come and out on to the main road. 'That was the local schoolteacher's house. I had to see him to ask for a loan of his wife.' Mark grinned wickedly at her surprised face. 'These West-Coasters are very generous. They'll give you anything, if you ask them nicely.'

'So it seems. Surely lending his wife is carrying generosity a bit far.'

'Oh, but he realized that my need was great.'

Judy knew he was laughing at her, so she kept quiet.

'I'd better explain. I went in to ask him if his wife would come and be chaperone tonight. Nan will be home tomorrow, but tonight it's a bit awkward. In a small country place like this you can't be too careful. If you stayed at home with just me and the twins I'd probably have to marry you to protect your good name.'

Judy appreciated his care of her. 'Thank you very much, but I can assure you that I wouldn't be asking you to make an honest woman out of me. You're quite safe. I hope I haven't been a nuisance arriving without warning, but I forgot to send a telegram this morning. Wouldn't it be better for me to stay at a hotel instead of bothering the school-teacher's wife?'

'Oh, it won't bother Claire MacLean. She's a real poppet. She said it will make Steve appreciate her more if he has to look after the kids tonight. Here we are.'

They turned off the main road, crossed the railway lines, and drove down a steep hill. When they stopped Mark carried her case and she followed him along a cement path and into a warm kitchen. As they entered Judy could hear children screaming. Mark dropped her case and ran.

He came back pushing two children in front of him.

'Do let me introduce you to your charges. This repulsive creature is Vicki and this equally repulsive little boy is Peter. They're ten years old. I told them to tidy up to meet you—and just look at them!'

Judy looked at the two bedraggled children and thought it better not to smile. But it was very hard to keep a straight face. They were both soaked to the skin and had some yellow gooey substance plastered on them. It was all through the little girl's long wet hair, while the little boy had a pair of scissors clutched in his hand. Both glared defiantly at her.

Mark gave them another shake. 'Well, explain yourselves. I told you to change and wash, and then I come back to find you like this. Peter, what were you doing with those scissors?'

'I was going to cut Vicki's hair,' Peter said flatly.

'He was too!' shrieked Vicki, twisting round, trying to aim a kick at Peter. 'He was going to cut all my hair off and make me bald!'

Mark looked exasperated. 'What in the world did you want to cut her hair for?'

'Because she broke my bantam's eggs.'

'This is becoming like a Mad Hatter's Tea Party,' said Mark grimly. 'Why did you break his bantam's eggs, Vicki?'

Vicki started to sob. 'B-because it said in a book that egg shampoo was good for washing hair and I wanted to look nice for the new lady.' She gave a hiccup. 'I only wanted two of them, and he bit me and I scratched him and he threw water over me and I threw the rest of the eggs at him and he tried to cut my hair off and I threw water at him and ...'

'That's enough,' roared Mark, 'that's more than enough! I don't know what I'll do with you. I'll let Judy deal with you.'

Judy risked a smile. 'Vicki is quite right, eggs are very good for hair, but not applied the way she's done it. Of course she should have asked Peter before taking them. Come and show me where the bathroom is, and I'll help you both clean up.'

Mark loosed his grip on the children. 'Now you know, Judy, why I mentioned you would have to have your health and strength unimpaired to deal with these two. I hope first impressions aren't lasting, because they really aren't bad little monsters usually.'

Judy hustled the children through the door to the bathroom. When she saw the mess they had made, she gasped.

'Well, you don't believe in doing things by halves, do you? We'll leave the bathroom till later. Which of you do I start on first?'

'I'll do myself,' announced Peter with great dignity. 'I'll go and have a shower in the wash-house while you do Vicki. Gee, isn't she a beaut mess?' He started to giggle.

'Take a look at yourself,' said Vicki indignantly. Then she started to laugh and Judy joined in. The three of them laughed until the tears ran down their faces. The ice was broken.

Judy recovered first. 'Peter, will you bring my case through from the kitchen? I'd better change.'

Vicki showed her to her room. She quickly slipped into a pair of trews and a jersey and hurried back to the bathroom with a bottle of egg-creme shampoo.

As she soaped and washed Vicki's hair, the little girl chatted non-stop. Judy cleaned the walls, while Vicki had a bath.

Judy followed Vicki back to the kitchen. It was a large, comfortable, but very untidy room. A cheerful fire was burning in the open fireplace and Mark was serving tea while Peter finished setting the table.

'Can I do anything to help?' Judy offered.

'No, certainly not,' replied Mark. 'You can be a guest tonight, but tomorrow I'll thankfully give up the role of chief cook and bottle-washer. Come on and sit up to the table.'

'Not stew again, Uncle Mark!' wailed Vicki.

'Stew again, yes. You know I can only cook stew and potatoes.' Then his blue eyes took on a mischievous twinkle. 'Actually, I was thinking of having scrambled eggs for a change.'

'Oh, that's not fair!' protested Peter, but he joined in the general laughter.

Judy enjoyed her tea very much, finding to her surprise that she was very hungry. She was very quiet, but enjoyed listening to the conversation and laughter of the others.

It was easy to see that there was a real bond of affection between the twins and their uncle. Also they shared a strong family resemblance. The three of them had the same startling blue eyes and dark good looks.

As they finished the meal a telephone rang somewhere in the house.

'Excuse me,' said Mark to Judy. 'You twins off to bed. There's school in the morning. Look sharp now,' and he went through to answer the telephone.

Judy started to clear the plates away to the sink.

'We'll help you do the dishes, Judy,' offered Vicki happily.

'No, we won't,' said Peter. 'Uncle Mark said we were to go to bed and he meant it. Good night, Judy. I'm glad we got someone nice like you.'

'Oh, so am I. I love having someone pretty and young. You ought to have seen the last one. A proper old bag, she was.' Vicki giggled at Judy's shocked face. 'Good night, Judy,' and she danced and whirled out through the door before Judy could think of admonishing her.

Judy cleared the table, then found some soap powder. She had half finished the dishes by the time Mark came back. He stood looking at her with a thoughtful expression on his face.

Judy became restless under his penetrating

gaze. She felt her face flush. 'What's the matter with me? Have I got a smudge on my face?'

'Oh no, your face is quite beautiful,' answered Mark, reaching for a tea towel. 'Just thinking what a lovely sight it is to see someone else washing the dishes.'

'Have you been without a housekeeper long?' asked Judy.

'Long enough. In fact, I'm sure I'm developing all the symptoms of housemaid's knee.'

Judy laughed. 'I'm sure you'll recover. Where do you keep the broom?'

'Leave the rest until the morning. Come and sit down by the fire. You've had a long trip. I meant to give the house a blitz before you arrived—however, you've seen us at our worst now. Are you still prepared to stay?'

'Yes, at least for the trial two weeks.'

'Good. That phone call was from Mother. I saw her this afternoon. I hope you don't mind that I told her all about you. She's looking forward to meeting you very much. She was so excited about coming home. I was worried in case you changed your mind. I told her I would pick her up at four o'clock tomorrow afternoon. She has to wait until the doctor does his rounds after lunch, or she would have insisted on me being there first thing in the morning.'

Mark stood up to get his cigarettes from the mantelpiece. 'I'll go through and see if the twins are asleep. I want to tell you about them.'

When he returned he sat down, his face was serious. 'I want to tell you this before Claire comes. I told you that Peter and Vicki are my brother Paul's children. Paul is a doctor. He specialized in tropical diseases. Early this year he had the most wonderful opportunity to go to South America to further his studies, and he took Betsy, his wife, with him. They left the twins here with me. Mother came with them to look after us all. Everyone knows that, but what I'm going to tell you now is only known to Mother and me. Whether you think we're right or wrong I want your word that you won't mention it to anyone, especially the twins.'

'You have my promise,' Judy said readily.

Mark nodded as if satisfied. 'They've been away eight months. Three months ago we had word from the leader of the party that Paul and Betsy had gone further into the interior with four native helpers, and that they had lost contact with the main camp.'

'Have you heard any further news since then?' asked Judy anxiously.

'Yes, but not good news.' Mark sighed. 'Six weeks ago we learnt that the native helpers had returned to the main camp. They said that Paul and Betsy had been in a canoe which had capsized, and that they were swept over a waterfall. The guides had searched the area but could find no trace of them. The man who wrote told us there was very little hope of them turning up alive after all this time. The country they were in was particularly wild and rugged. Even if they had got ashore, they would have been without guides, and without their equipment. There are mosquitoes, snakes, dangerous swamps, not to mention hostile natives.'

Judy was appalled. How petty her worries were compared to what this family was facing! 'What a terrible time for you. No wonder your mother was under a strain,' she said sympathetically.

'Yes, it's been pretty rough on her,' Mark agreed. 'We decided in the beginning to keep it from the twins. Why worry them when there may be no need? Then when we received the next letter we did not know what to do for the best. I just can't believe that Paul and Betsy are dead, and Mother feels the same way. After all, their bodies weren't found, even by the party that went out from the main camp. Somehow I feel that they'll turn up. The leader of the expedition said he'll come and see us when they return to New Zealand at Christmas. So until then Mother and I have decided to say nothing to the twins. Perhaps it's just cowardice, that I can't bear to tell them, but I don't think so. Paul and Betsy were capable, physically and mentally, of dealing with any emergency. I won't give up hope yet.'

Judy did not know what to say to comfort him. 'I'm inclined to believe that they're safe,' she said slowly. 'Especially as your mother feels the same way as you do. Mothers seem to have a sixth sense as far as their children are concerned. There were so many stories during the war proving that they do. I've heard of mothers knowing the hour their sons died, days before the War Office notified them, and if your mother feels that Paul is still alive, then I think you were right not to tell Peter and Vicki.'

'Thanks, Judy. Your sympathy has helped. Of course the twins are disappointed that they haven't had any letters for so long, but they think it's because of the trip. We try to act as natural as possible, otherwise they would be quick to notice we were worried. It hasn't been easy, I can tell you.'

They heard a car stop at the gate. Mark stood up. 'That will be Claire, I'll go and bring her in.'

Judy liked Claire as soon as she met her. Claire was small and fair with lovely brown eyes which danced with fun.

'I think I must really be on the scrap heap when I get asked to play chaperone! Steve says I'm too flighty for the job, but he's only worried that if the kids cry he'll have to get up to them.'

Judy laughed. 'How many children have

you got?'

'Two little darlings, Jane is three and Robin is two. You tell her, Mark, aren't they wonderful children?'

'Oh, quite wonderful,' Mark agreed with a smile. 'Exceptional children, Judy, they really are. They never cry, never get cross, never fight, always go to sleep when they're told . . .'

'Stop it! You're not fair,' Claire cried. 'They're not angels, I admit that, but they're nicer than anyone else's kids, so there!'

'And there you have a completely genuine, unbiased opinion,' teased Mark.

Judy laughed; she could see these two were very good friends. It amazed her to see Mark smiling and happy as if he didn't have a care in the world. Only minutes before he had been so serious, so genuinely concerned about his brother. She realized how much easier it would have been for him and his mother if their friends knew the trouble they were in. They would be offered plenty of sympathy, she was sure, but if too many people knew there was always the chance that someone would speak out of turn in front of the twins. She admired their courage.

Judy, Claire and Mark had coffee, and were all happy to retire early.

Although Judy was very tired, she found it hard to get to sleep. She kept thinking of the twins. Poor little children, waiting every day to hear from their parents, quite unaware that they might never see them again. What a nice person Claire was. She looked far too young to be married with two children. She thought of Mark. Which was his true character? One side was lighthearted, teasing and acting like the charming idiot, and the other was serious, sensitive and compassionate.

CHAPTER IV

The next two weeks passed as if on wings. Judy decided to spring-clean the house. The weather was beautifully fine. She washed, scrubbed and polished. The house had been remodelled inside and out just before Mark had taken over, so by the time Judy finished turning out the cupboards and drawers of each room, and washing the covers and curtains, the whole house sparkled.

Judy loved Mrs Palmer. As she worked from room to room they talked and discussed every subject under the sun. Judy had known at the first meeting that she was going to like her. As each day passed the bond of friendship strengthened. Mrs Palmer's wise kindly eyes followed the trim energetic figure as she moved deftly from one task to another. She understood from listening to Judy more than the girl realized of the loneliness of her adolescent years and of her longing to find a place of her own.

Judy accepted joyfully the warmth, love and understanding that Mrs Palmer offered her.

One evening after Judy had supervised the twins going to bed she put the ironing blanket on the table and switched on the iron.

'Judy dear, leave that until tomorrow. You're doing far too much,' Mrs Palmer protested.

Judy laughed gaily. 'I'm not; I'm just loving it here. When I do this ironing and put it away we'll have finished the spring-cleaning.'

'*We* will have finished,' replied Mrs Palmer. 'Very nice of you to include me when you wouldn't let me do a hand's turn. You've worked like a Trojan. The whole house looks lovely, fresh and clean and sweet. It was a lucky day for this family, the day Mark met you.'

'Lucky for me, you mean,' Judy said. 'Do you know, I've hardly ever lived in a house— I mean, been part of a household. And you've let me do just what I liked. After years of boarding schools and living in hospital nursing homes this has been a wonderful experience.'

Mrs Palmer smiled at Judy's bright flushed face. This gay, lively young girl had lifted such a load off her shoulders. The twins adored her, and no wonder. She was marvellous with them.

'Did Mark say what time he would be home?'

Judy paused in her work and looked at the clock, 'Oh, he shouldn't be long. He said the meeting would finish about ten. Would you like to go to bed now?'

'No, I had a rest this afternoon. I'll stay up and have supper with you when he comes in. Have you much more to do?'

'I've nearly finished,' Judy answered, switching off the iron. 'Tomorrow I'm going to start on the garden.'

'You'll do nothing of the sort, Judy. You've worked so hard since you arrived, you'll have to take a day off for a rest. Now I insist. The garden can wait, I feel so ashamed just sitting around doing nothing. Tomorrow I'm going to do the cooking while you have one complete day free.'

'We'll see,' Judy said soothingly.

'There's the car. That will be Mark home.' Mrs Palmer put the kettle on. 'I'm making supper to show my independence. Don't you "we'll see" me, madam. You'll make me think I'm back in the hospital!'

They were still laughing when Mark came in. Judy picked up the pile of freshly ironed clothes and put them in the cupboard.

'How did the meeting go, Mark?' his mother asked.

'Okay. Much the same as usual. They need some younger men in the executive positions. I think there'll be a shake-up at the next annual meeting. What were you two laughing about?'

'Judy has been bullying me, Mark,' complained his mother, handing him a cup of tea. 'Now sit down, Judy, here's your tea.'

'You can see who's doing the bullying, can't you, Mark?' Judy said as she meekly accepted her tea.

'Don't let her get the upper hand, Judy. She's a very wicked old lady. Too fond of getting her own way altogether, aren't you, Nan?'

'Wait until you hear what I'm arguing about before you take sides, Mark,' said his mother firmly as she joined them by the fire. 'Judy has been working hard ever since she arrived. I want her to take the day off to-morrow. She wants to do the garden.'

'Your mother wants to take over the cooking and you asked me here to see she didn't work too hard, so you can decide.'

'Not me. You can fight it out between you. My money will be on Nan. She's had years of experience, and is very skilled at defeating her opponents in the most devious ways. Aren't you, pet?'

'Yes,' admitted Mrs Palmer complacently, and they all laughed together.

As Judy got ready for bed that night she thought how wonderful it was that she fitted into the household so easily. Mrs Palmer was a dear. The twins were mischievous but lovable. And Mark—Judy shied away from investigating her thoughts on Mark.

Bruce had written three letters. She must answer him. But what could she say? She had been so busy it had been relatively easy to push the problem of their relationship away to the back of her mind. She sat in bed with a pen in her hand staring at a blank page. Finally she wrote a newsy letter of all her doings over the last two weeks, signed it and sealed the envelope.

Poor Bruce, he would search the letter for some personal message, but he would look in vain. She was not ready to come to any decision. Life was so free and uncomplicated in this warm, friendly household. She had no desire to pitchfork herself back into the strained battle of trying to reach a decision.

Some day soon she would discuss her problem with Mrs Palmer. Strange how neither Mark nor his mother had questioned her as to the outcome of her meeting with Bruce. She appreciated their attitude of waiting until she was willing to talk. The friendliness of their welcome, the approval they showed of the work she did, and the genuine pleasure they took from her company soothed her after the buffeting she had received from Bruce's mother.

She snuggled down in her comfortable bed, content and relaxed.

The next morning she found that Mrs Palmer was in control of the kitchen, and had no intention of being displaced.

' It won't hurt me to do the cooking, Judy. Go over to the shed and watch Mark milking the cows.'

Judy wandered out into the bright sunshine. It was a beautiful morning. How close the snow-capped mountains looked. The Southern Alps dominated the whole scene. She walked down the lawn to the little creek and gazed into the water.

The children had some pet eels and were always begging the scraps to feed them on. The twins were very proud of them, but Judy thought they were horrible. As she watched a huge eel slid through the water and nosed against the bank expectantly. Judy shuddered. There was something repulsive about the long snake-like body. How the children could like them she would never know. They even named the wretched things, and they laughed at Judy for being scared of them.

'Come on, Judy, we're going to feed the calves. Come and help us,' called Vicki.

'She's not to help, Vicki—just watch. You know Nan said she was on holiday today,' Peter said.

'I'd love to watch,' answered Judy, catching up with them. 'I wouldn't be much help anyway, Vicki. I've never been on a farm before.'

'Oh, I'll show you what to do. It's easy,' replied Vicki importantly.

Judy followed them across the yard to the cowshed. Her interested eyes took in the big concrete yard, the pipe rail fence, the white-painted walls, and the gleaming stainless steel pipes. Everything was spotlessly clean. Mark did not notice her by the wall. A radio was playing the latest pop music and the twins were busy collecting some small buckets.

Judy watched Mark move from one bail to the next. The cows were black and white. They looked enormous to Judy. Mark moved swiftly yet quietly amongst them. She saw the pattern of work emerging. Let one cow go, put the machines on the next, wash the cow that had walked into the empty bail and take a few squirts of milk from it, move on to another bail, let the cow go, back and put the machines on the washed cow. Judy was fascinated. It looked so easy, so effortless, but Judy was not deceived. Mark looked up and smiled, 'Hullo, what do you think of my cows? Beauties, aren't they?' He patted one cow that was standing ready for a bail. 'This is Lucy, my pride and joy. Wait until the herd-tester comes. You're going to be the best cow in the district this year, aren't you, my pet?'

He changed several more machines and then came through to the small room beside Judy. He pulled a full can of milk away against the wall and put a new one under the cooler. The children came in. 'The calves are ready, Uncle Mark,' Vicki yelled above the noise of the machines and music.

'Right, go on with the shed. I'll be a few minutes before I can carry the milk out.'

Judy was astonished as the twins went into the main yard and carried on with the work.

The children were so quick, so capable, and yet so small.

'Want to have a go?' Judy jumped; she had not heard Mark walk up beside her. 'No, thanks, I couldn't do that—I'd be too scared. Do the cows like the latest pop songs?'

'Of course they do. Actually it makes them much quieter; they don't jump at every sound—and strange voices don't affect them.'

Judy followed the twins out to the calf pens. She watched the children get the buckets of milk ready and then bring in the smallest calves first.

'These are the youngest,' explained Peter. 'They're still on fresh milk. The next lot are on half and half, half fresh milk and half skim milk, that is, with a little oil, and the bigger ones have skim milk, oil and mash.'

The calves were quickly fed and put back in their paddock. The twins scrubbed the buckets and put them in a rack.

'Come on, Judy, we're going home now, or we'll miss the school bus,' Vicki told Judy.

'She's staying with me,' said Mark. 'Now off you go. Thanks for the help.'

'Judy's our friend,' Vicki protested. 'Me and Peter brought her over. You're not fair!'

'No, I'm not fair, I'm very dark,' laughed Mark. 'Now scat. Quick!' As the children ran off he said, 'Come and sit in the sun by the water trough while I finish up.'

Mark milked the last of the cows and put

them out, then hosed down the yard and rails. He washed and sterilized the machines, then went into the side-room and put the milk cans in the huge wall-length refrigerator. Judy was content to sit in the warm sun and listen to the pleasant music while she watched his quick, energetic, methodical movements. In an astonishingly short time the cleaning up was done.

Mark grinned down at her. 'I'm sure you've enjoyed watching me work and are full of admiration for my supremely efficient methods.'

Judy, who had been doing just that, said primly, 'Oh, I'd heard the Colonials had no little conceit of themselves.'

'Oh, had you? Did you also hear that we don't like being called Colonials and that we're wild and reckless, especially when insulted before breakfast?' Without effort he scooped her into his arms and held her poised over the water trough. 'Apologize or I'll drop you in!'

Judy struggled wildly. 'Let me down! You wouldn't dare!'

'Oh, wouldn't I?' His blue eyes were full of mischief. He lowered her feet into the water. 'Say sorry like a lady for calling me a big skite. One, two, three!'

'I'm sorry!' Judy yelled.

Mark set her carefully on her feet. 'Thank you for your most abject apology.'

63

'You're no gentleman,' stormed Judy. 'You hurt me.'

'I did not,' replied Mark, smiling, and held the gate open with exaggerated courtesy. 'Let's go home and get some breakfast. Come on, Judy love, I don't like fighting on an empty stomach. Don't sulk.'

'Oh, you're impossible,' replied Judy, but she smiled as she went through the gate beside him. It was extraordinary. If any other man had treated her like that she would have marched off in high dudgeon. But Mark seemed to be able to tease her, make her fighting mad, then disarm her completely with that wonderful smile of his.

After breakfast Judy tidied and cleaned the bedrooms, and as Nan still would not let her into the kitchen, she wandered out into the garden. How lovely it was! The huge lawn, swept down to the creek which was bordered by a mass of golden daffodils. Two huge rhododendron trees were just coming into bud. Some forsythia trees were in bloom with their shower of golden bells; and the heavenly scent of a heavily laden daphne tree filled the air.

Nan joined her. 'There's just a small patch of garden to weed, Judy. Here along the cement path. Mac does the lawns and shrubs, also the vegetable garden.'

'Who is Mac?'

'He's an old man who lives across the

road. He's a grand old chap, Mr McTaggart, but he takes a lot of knowing. He keeps the place looking lovely.'

'Yes, it really is beautiful. I wondered how Mark found time to do the lawns.'

'Oh, Mark!' laughed Nan. 'He would rather plough and sow a hundred acres than do a small vegetable garden. Mac has been here as long as I can remember. He taught both Mark and Paul to fish and last year he taught Peter. They're both eagerly looking forward to the fishing season which starts in October.'

While Nan went inside, Judy got busy with her gardening fork. It took her about an hour to weed and dig the small garden. She was busy admiring her work when around the corner came an old man. He was tall, straight and almost gaunt, and his hair was snow-white. He eyed Judy up and down, then looked at the garden.

'You've no done a bad job there, lassie.'

'Thank you.' Judy brushed her hair back from her forehead. 'Are you Mr McTaggart?'

The old man nodded. 'And you'll be Judy. The children have been telling me of you.'

'You like gardening, Mr McTaggart?'

'Yes.' The soft Scottish burr was most apparent.

'How long have you been in New Zealand? You haven't lost your accent.'

'I have no kept track of the years. I came

here as a young lad of eighteen to seek my fortune.'

'And did you find it?'

'No, but I found something a lot better—contentment.'

'What part of Scotland do you come from?'

'I was born in Skye. The Isle of Skye.'

'Why, isn't that strange! I was on Skye last year. I went with a friend on a trip to Scotland last year and went to several of the islands.'

The old man's keen eyes brightened and he questioned Judy eagerly on the changes that had come to the Island since he was there last.

'Have you ever been back, Mr McTaggart?'

'Oh yes, I went back. I had no been in New Zealand only but a few years when the war broke out, and I went to France. Spent four years in the trenches there. I went to Skye on leave, and a great fuss of me they made.'

Nan came to the door. 'Cup of tea, Judy. Oh, good morning, Mac. Come and have a cup of tea with us?'

'No, thank you, missus. I'll be away to my work,' and he walked briskly away.

As Judy and Mrs Palmer sat down for their tea Mark walked in.

'My word, you ladies do yourselves proud. Every time I come in you're sitting gossiping over a cup of tea,' he teased.

'For that you can get your own cup of tea,' said Nan firmly. 'Judy has been working hard in the garden this morning.'

'I met Mr McTaggart,' Judy offered.

'I'll bet that didn't take long. Mac would say "Good morning" and that would be that. He's one of the strong silent types like myself.'

'Oh, I wouldn't say that. He talked to me for ages. I think he's a real poppet.'

'Ye gods!' cried Mark. 'If he hears you calling him a poppet you'd better look out.'

'It's true, Mark,' said Nan. 'She had old Mac eating out of her hand. I looked out and saw them going hammer and tongs, so I waited a while before I called them.'

'Our Judy is quite a girl. One look from her and we men are down on our knees.'

It wasn't so much what he said but the look in his eyes that made Judy blush.

'Now, Mark, you just stop teasing Judy,' said Nan sternly. 'Have another scone, Judy, you earned it.'

'What are you doing with yourself after lunch, Judy? Would you like to come for a walk around the farm with me?'

'Why, I'd love to.' Judy's face lit up with pleasure. 'But what about you, Nan?'

'Now stop worrying, I'm fine. I'll go to bed for a rest after lunch—that's a promise. You go with Mark. The walk will do you good. You've been tied to the house ever since you arrived.' Nan patted Judy's hand affectionately.

'Watch her, Judy. She's a very cunning old lady. She knows you've been here two weeks and she's worked you like a slave. Now she's trying to sweeten you up in case you've decided to up stakes and leave us to it.'

'Oh, I wouldn't do that. I love it here. I mean—that is,' Judy blushed and stammered, 'if you want me to stay.'

'Want you to stay?' Mark grinned. 'Nan and I were discussing the purchase of a ball and chain—'

'Shh, don't be ridiculous, Mark. Judy my dear, of course we want you to stay. I can't tell you the difference it's made to the whole family having you here. We were at our lowest ebb. I was becoming so depressed, lying in hospital, worrying about Mark and the children, about Paul and Betsy, and then Mark brought you home.'

'Not bad for a pick-up, is she, Nan?' Mark's smile was wicked.

'Out of here, Mark! Out you go! I'm ashamed of you.' Nan chased him out the door and shut it firmly behind him. 'I'm sorry, Judy. Mark shouldn't tease like that.' that.'

'Don't worry, I'm not offended.' Judy giggled. 'I think he's a proper nut.'

* * *

After lunch she walked down the farm road with Mark. The sun was shining, the gorse was in bloom, the grass green—it was glorious.

Mark explained, 'This road we're on was originally the main road. When the railway came through they built the main road on a higher level. Suits me fine having a good road from one end of the farm to the other, the bridges thrown in too. I don't know where I'd be without it when the farm floods. I have to bring all the stock up here.'

Judy, who had been looking with interest at the green fields sloping gently down to a river in the distance, turned incredulously. 'You mean a flood could cover all your farm?'

'It has many times,' Mark answered.

'You're joking again.'

'I'm telling the truth, Judy love, and it's no joke. You remember the name of the station the night you arrived?'

Judy nodded. 'Stillwater.'

'Yes, Stillwater. Well, below Stillwater, on the way to Greymouth, there's a gorge—very narrow—with sheer rock walls. When it rains for two or three days—heavy rain, I mean— the water from back country creeks and rivers comes roaring down the Grey. It can't get through the gorge quickly enough, so it backs up and up. This farm, except for this road and the house, goes completely under water. Not a raging flood water, still and quiet, but just as deadly.'

'It must be horrible,' Judy shuddered, feeling cold in spite of the sun.

'It's not that bad really,' replied Mark. 'I've got friends who live up country. When the river there bursts the banks in a big flood they ring me and I know I've got about four hours to clear the stock. I was caught badly the first year I was here, but I'm a bit more careful now. You'll probably see a flood one of these days.'

'I don't want to,' Judy answered hurriedly.

'Neither do I want one, but we usually get a good flood in September or October. Of course, plenty of times I move the stock and it's only a false alarm, but if I don't move quickly at the first sign then they're cut off. See how those deep gullies run through the farm. The water fills those first then gradually covers the farm. When I own it, I'm going to bridge those gullies and I won't be forced to clear the stock every small flood.'

'When will you own the farm?' asked Judy.

'The beginning of March is D-Day. At the moment I lease it from my uncle's estate, but in five months' time it should be mine, God willing.'

'I wouldn't want to own it if half the time it's under water.'

'How you women love to exaggerate—half

the time! Sometimes there isn't a big flood in two or three years. Sometimes it can go under water three times in one week, but the point is all the best land on the Coast is near the river. Anyway, the water only stays about twelve hours at the outside.'

They walked down off the road and crossed a little bridge. The scent of the blue gums was strong and tangy. Judy crushed the leaves in her fingers.

'See those big pines there on the hill? They're over a hundred years old. The first settler on this farm planted them.'

Judy loved her walk around the farm and noticed the pride in Mark's voice as he showed her his stock—the sheep, the calves, the yearlings, the two-year-old steers, and, as they came in a full circle back to the house, the black and white dairy cows, sleek and healthy.

'I've been all over the farm,' she boasted to Nan and the twins at afternoon tea.

'That you haven't,' interrupted Mark. 'You've seen about half of it. I've three hundred acres across the creek to the north. It's pretty rough up there. A lot of it's swamp and flax and bush. I'll take you that way next time.'

'Hurry up and finish your tea,' begged Peter. 'Then you can come and get the cows with us.'

'No, Judy has done enough walking today.

She's too tired to go for the cows with you—another time perhaps,' Mark said firmly.

Judy, who had been feeling tired after walking for hours, could not bear to see the disappointment on the twins' faces.

Vicki, always the most aggressive, was arguing. ' You had her all day, Uncle Mark. You showed her all your mouldy old farm, and when we want to show her our things you say she's too tired. You're mean. You said Judy came to look after us and now you're keeping her for yourself.'

Judy laughed, and felt a warm glow of happiness at being wanted. It wiped away her fatigue. ' I'm not a bit tired. Get Nan's gumboots out again and I'll be there in a minute.'

The twins showed her all their favourite places on the way down for the cows—the pond where they caught tadpoles, a tree hut they had built last summer, a wild duck's nest. When they returned to the shed Mark had the motor going and the twins wanted to teach Judy how to milk the cows.

' No!' Mark was firm. ' Judy is tired, she's going to sit by the water trough and look delectable, while you two show her what good workers you are.'

' Why can't I learn?' questioned Judy.

' Because I'm not having you getting hurt while you're here. It's not as easy as it looks. Now go and sit down out of the way.'

'If a little girl of ten can do it, I don't see why I can't.'

'*Go and sit down!*'

Judy was really rather relieved and did what she was told. Later, during a pause in the milking, Peter sidled up to her and whispered, 'Uncle Mark's just being stuffy. Me and Vicki will show you how to milk at the weekend. We won't let him know until you can do it real good.'

Judy, who had only argued with Mark because she was tired and feeling contrary, rather than that she had any real desire to learn how to milk, wondered what she had let herself in for. She was thankful that the twins had confidence in her ability, but realized that she would have to do the work, or they would think she was letting the side down.

Later on that evening after the twins were in bed Mark suddenly realized that he had left the gate behind the orchard open. He went out to the back door, then returned. 'Come for a walk down to the orchard with me, Judy. There's a beautiful full moon. I'll bet you've never seen anything like it.'

'I'm comfortable here, thanks,' Judy replied.

'Look, Mark, you've walked the poor girl off her feet today. Leave her in peace.'

'She's just lazy,' Mark coaxed. 'Come on, Judy. It's such a beautiful night I want to share it with someone.'

Judy went through to her room and put on a jacket and shoes. They walked in silence down to the orchard. Mark closed the gate and they leaned on it as they looked at the sky.

'Thank you for making me come, Mark,' Judy said softly. 'I've never seen the moon so big. It's magnificent, the snow on the mountains shining in the moonlight and the scent of the blossoms. I can't find the words to describe it. Those mountains seem to call me. One day I'd like to try climbing them.'

Suddenly from the tree above her came the most horrible chuckling—like the laugh of a madman.

'Mark!' screamed Judy, and threw herself into his arms, terrified. Mark's arms closed around her as he roared with laughing.

'What are you laughing at? What was that horrible noise?' demanded Judy indignantly, trying to release herself.

'That was only an opossum up the plum tree, Judy. Now stand still and tell me, did you mean what you said to Nan this morning about wanting to stay here?'

'Yes. Let me go.'

'What about Bruce? Are you still going to marry him?'

'I don't know. I told him I'd think it over and that's what I'm doing. There's no hurry. Let me go.'

'One more question. At this moment, then,

you're not engaged to Bruce?'

'No.' The sensation of being held in Mark's strong arms was making Judy feel very peculiar.

'Good,' replied Mark, and bent and kissed her competently and enthusiastically, then quietly released her.

'How dare you kiss me?' demanded Judy angrily.

'No trouble. You launched yourself into my arms—I mean I'd be a fool not to avail myself of the opportunity. At least I checked to see if you were free first. I think I was very helpful.'

'Helpful?' spluttered Judy indignantly.

'Yes, helpful. You said you were trying to make up your mind whether to marry Bruce or not. Well, now you know what it might be like if you don't marry him.'

'You haven't helped at all—you've made me more confused.'

'In what way?' asked Mark innocently.

'Never mind. I'm going home.'

'Don't be mad, Judy love, I'll behave myself. Come and see the little chap who frightened you.'

Judy let him lead her forward to see the furry little opossum. It peered down at her with bright inquisitive eyes. 'Oh, isn't he a darling? I'd love to cuddle him.'

'Well, don't,' advised Mark. 'They have very strong, sharp claws.' Taking her hand in his warm comforting clasp, he walked slowly home. 'Have you enjoyed your day off, Judy?'

'Very much, but I'm tired.'

'You'll sleep well tonight. I want to add my thanks to Nan's—it's been wonderful having you here. Bless your generous heart for coming. It's not only the work you've done, but you've brought laughter and light —the whole atmosphere has changed. I can now concentrate on the farm without worrying about Nan and the kids.'

At the steps he released her hand and turned to face her. He looked at her steadily for a few moments and Judy felt oddly breathless. His hand came up and gently traced the outline of her face.

'You're very beautiful, Judy. You have much to offer a man. Take your time deciding your future. Don't waste yourself on a man who's not worthy of your love.' Then he smiled. 'Sermon over for tonight, off you go to bed. I'll sit here and have a smoke before I go in. Good night.'

'Good night, Mark.' Judy hurried inside. She could not get away from him quickly enough. He disturbed her. Nan had gone to bed. Judy quickly washed and undressed. Before she got into bed she looked in the mirror... Beautiful? No, she wasn't beautiful, but her face was flushed and her eyes were shining like a child who had just seen a Christmas tree.

Angrily she switched off the light. Darn it all, what was the matter with her? Two weeks ago she was breaking her heart over Bruce and now she was all of a quiver because Mark had told her she was beautiful. Her heart couldn't be trusted—she must be a very fickle, shallow-minded girl.

She tried to think of Bruce, but before her was the image of Mark's deep blue eyes and his teasing, tantalizing smile. All right then, admit it. He was an exciting person to be with—she couldn't ignore him—he was so vital, so attractive so—so—so comforting somehow. That slow sweet smile would be her undoing if she wasn't careful. He was only her employer—he meant nothing to her, just her boss—she meant nothing to him. She must keep it that way. Her life had enough complications without adding any more.

CHAPTER V

'Are you going to see Uncle Mark play football, Judy?' asked Peter on Saturday morning. 'It's the last game of the season. If his team wins this match, they'll win the competition. It will be a great game.'

'I don't know a thing about football, Peter.'

'I'll go with you, Judy, and tell you what's going on. Uncle Mark is a beaut player,' Peter told her earnestly.

'He's the best in the world,' cried Vicki with her usual enthusiasm.

'No, Vicki, that's not true—the All Blacks are the best in the world. Don Clark—'

'Blow Don Clark. Uncle Mark is the best.'

Peter, who took his football seriously, was annoyed. 'Oh, girls! They don't know anything,' and he ran off.

'I do! I do! I know everything,' screamed Vicki, racing after him.

Judy smiled. It was amazing what different natures they had considering they were twins. Vicki was volatile, excitable, and imaginative while Peter was steady, responsible and thoughtful, but both possessed a lively sense of fun.

After lunch time Mark said to Judy with a quizzical expression on his face, 'I hear you won't want to live if you can't come and see me play football.'

Judy was stopped from a hasty denial by the anxious pleading look on Peter's face. So that was it! Peter was using her to get to the football match.

'Well, I don't think I put it quite as strongly as that, but yes, I would like to see you play.'

'Do you know anything about football?' Mark asked.

'Just that the All Blacks are the best in the world. Peter has promised to come and explain the game to me.'

'That's a good boy, Peter,' teased Mark. 'Giving up a whole Saturday afternoon to teach Judy the rudiments of the game.'

Peter's honest face flushed. 'I wanted to go too, Uncle Mark.'

'Well, so you shall. Do you want to go too, Nan? Vicki?'

'Not me,' replied Nan flatly. 'I hate football. Great big men chasing a little ball and getting their clothes in such a mess.'

'Nan, you're a shocker, a disgrace to New Zealand. However, we'll see if we can make a convert out of Judy.'

'I'm going too,' shouted Vicki. 'I'm going to see Uncle Mark play. He's the best in the world, aren't you, Uncle Mark?'

'Oh, without doubt,' Mark laughed, picking the little girl up and tossing her in the air, to her wild delight.

Peter took his task seriously, and while

they waited in the grandstand for the game to start, he carefully explained the rules to Judy.

'Here they are now, Judy,' he said. 'Uncle Mark is the one out in front. He's the Captain. See, his team wears red jerseys. The others wear green.'

Once the game started Judy felt herself caught up in the excitement. The supporters of both teams were extremely vocal and the candid comments would have made some of the players' ears burn if they could have heard.

At half time the score was even, eight all. The air was tense. Then the green team scored a try but failed to convert it, making the score eleven-eight. Peter's face was grim.

'You wait, Uncle Mark's team will win.'

Personally Judy thought it doubtful. Time and time again Mark's team were pressing on the goal line, but each time the green team's defence was too good. Then, just in the closing seconds of the game, Mark took the ball on his own twenty-five and started to run. He raced down the field, over half-way, side-stepped two men and was still going. He was over the twenty-five and stepped out of a tackle. The crowd were on their feet yelling. He had only one man to beat. He ran straight at him, then swerved at the last minute. Judy found herself on her feet screaming 'Mark, Mark!' with Peter and

Vicki as he touched down for a try.

The crowd cheered and cheered. It had been a magnificent run. Then they hushed as he went back to take the kick.

'I don't know if he can do it,' Peter muttered anxiously. 'It's not an easy kick. Oh, I hope he does.'

Mark stood up from placing the ball, then stepped back several paces and ran in and kicked. It soared up beautifully high and straight, directly between the posts.

His supporters went wild. As the referee's whistle went for full time they poured out on the field.

'Oh boy, oh boy! Isn't he beaut, Judy?' cried Peter.

'See, I told you Uncle Mark was the best,' Vicki spoke with smug satisfaction. 'The best in the world. Wasn't he wonderful?'

'He certainly was,' agreed Judy, smiling. The twins were apparently among Mark's most ardent admirers.

They made their way out to the car to wait for Mark.

'He won't be long, Judy. He has to shower and change. Oh, that was a real good game. Are you glad you came?' Peter asked.

'Very glad.'

When Mark arrived the twins were all over him. He started the car and pulled out into the traffic. 'Well, Judy, what did you think of your first game of football?'

'I really enjoyed it. It was tremendously exciting, especially your try. I'm sorry I won't be able to see any more games.'

'Well, not this season. It's all finished for this year. The boys are throwing a party to-night. Would you like to go along with me? It will be a good show.'

'I'd love—' Judy stopped suddenly, re-membering her resolution not to get involved. 'Sorry, Mark, I don't think I should.' It was hard to say.

'Second thoughts aren't always the best, Judy.'

'Perhaps not, but—'

Vicki burst in indignantly, 'I think you're mean, not going to the party with Uncle Mark.'

'That will do, Vicki,' Mark said firmly. 'Judy has a friend in Christchurch. He might be very angry if she went out with me.'

'I bet he's not as nice as Uncle Mark.' Vicki was not pacified.

'Now, now, Vicki, don't be rude,' said Mark.

Peter suddenly joined in, 'If Zelda doesn't mind you going out with Judy, Uncle Mark, why should her friend mind?'

'That will do, you two—shut up and sit quiet. See, down there, Judy, that's the gorge I was telling you about. Remember, the one that causes the flooding.'

That evening when Mark went out Judy regretted that she had refused to go with him. The house suddenly seemed quiet and dull. Who was Zelda? She would have liked to ask Nan, but did not want to appear interested. he must have a girl then. Zelda—what an interesting name. Of course someone as attractive as Mark wouldn't be unattached at his age. She tried to ignore the flat feeling of disappointment. Why should she care?

'Come on, twins—I'll give you a game of draughts. I'm feeling lucky tonight. Last time we played you both beat me. Tonight it will be different.'

The twins were enjoying coaching Judy in the milking shed. Whenever Mark left them alone in the shed, Peter made Judy bail up to the cows and then gradually she learnt to wash them and use the strip cup and finally to change the machines.

The first time she put on the machines she did it perfectly. The next time it was a disaster. She fumbled about until she lost all the vacuum and all the machines in the shed fell off. Vicki, who was on guard watching for Mark, raced in and hissed, 'Get back by the trough—here's Uncle Mark. We'll take the blame.'

Mark scolded them for being so careless and helped them put the machines back on. The twins giggled conspiratorially. Judy did not want to try again, but they bullied her into it. Soon she was almost as proficient as they were in the shed.

Each day after they went to school Judy helped Mark scrub up the shed.

One evening when Mark failed to return at milking time the twins and Judy brought the cows in, set up the shed and started the milking. By the time Mark arrived hot and bothered just on dark they were finishing off.

As it happened the twins were out feeding the calves and Judy was coping single-handed with the shed. She already had the separator turned on for the excess milk.

Mark stared in astonishment. 'Where did you learn to milk?'

Judy grinned at him impishly. 'Ask the twins! They thought I was upset because you wouldn't let me learn to milk, so they decided to teach me on the side.'

'Wow, what a surprise! You're really one out of the box, Judy. Where are those kids anyway?'

'Out feeding the calves. Here they are now. Look, if you aren't going to help, get out of the way so we can finish off. Go and sit on the water trough so you don't get hurt.'

The twins laughed uproariously. 'Serve you right, Uncle Mark,' jeered Peter. 'We knew she could do it.'

Judy let the last line of cows go and started hosing down the shed, while the twins pumped the water through. Mark took charge of the separator room.

'I'm amazed, downright amazed. How did you learn to set up the machines—the separator?'

Judy was quite nonchalant. 'You don't think I've been sitting here with my eyes shut for the last six weeks, do you? I've helped you dismantle the darned thing every morning, so I just reversed the order. Easy!'

'Well, I'll be damned. What a great bunch of kids you are! I came home really had it, thinking I'd be all hours getting finished, and here I find you've done all the work. You are proper marvels.'

The twins revelled in his praise. At dinner time they shared the joke with Nan and became over-excited, but no one wanted to spoil their fun. The twins delayed going to bed trying to extend the happiness of the evening.

'Wait until I go home to England and tell my friends I milked a whole herd of cows. They'll never believe me,' said Judy.

'You're not going home, are you?' asked Vicki anxiously.

'Not yet, not for a long time,' Judy soothed.

'Why don't you stay here—I mean for always?' Peter suggested.

'Oh, I couldn't do that. Some day I'll have to leave, but I'll always remember this farm and the happy times I've had here.'

Peter persisted, 'You mean when Mum

and Dad come home, and Nan and Vicki and me go back to Dunedin.'

'Yes, I'll have to leave then,' replied Judy, smiling at their eager faces.

'Why don't you marry Uncle Mark? Then you could stay,' Peter wanted to know.

'Now that is an idea, Peter,' Mark laughed. 'I wonder I didn't think of it myself. She can cook—she's not bad-looking and now you've taught her to milk she'd be invaluable. Yes, I must consider it.'

Vicki danced up and down, 'Yes, do, Uncle Mark, then we can keep her.' Then her face fell. 'Oh no, you can't. You've got to marry Zelda so you can get all that money.'

There was a sudden shocked silence. Judy did not know where to look—Vicki, now aware that something was wrong, started to cry.

'Where did you hear that bit of news, Vicki? Have you been listening at the door when Nan and I were talking? You're a very naughty little girl—you need a good thrashing!' Judy had never seen him so angry.

Vicki, now thoroughly upset, screamed, 'I didn't listen at the door. I hate you! I hate you!' and she ran from the room sobbing bitterly.

'Do you know what she was talking about, Peter?' Mark demanded.

'Yes, I do,' shouted Peter fiercely, 'and I think you're rotten. Vicki came out one night for a drink ages ago, and you and Nan were talking. The door was open. She came and told me, something about a will. If you'd shut the door she wouldn't have heard. I wish—I wish Mum and Dad would come home. I hate it here! He burst into tears and ran out, slamming the door behind him.

Judy was shocked that Peter should cry. He was such a tough, hardy little boy. She had seen him get some really sore hurts without making a fuss. Poor little fellow, he must be very upset.

Nan stood up, obviously very distressed. 'The poor little things! What a pity when they were so pleased with themselves. I must go and comfort them.'

'Nan, do you think they could have heard us discussing Paul and Betsy? How could we have been so damned careless? I feel sick at the thought.'

'Now, Mark, don't worry. I'm sure they wouldn't have kept it to themselves if they'd heard us discussing Paul and Betsy. They would have asked questions.'

'Then go through and talk to them, Nan—I'll come and make my peace later. Poor little brats. I shouldn't have jumped at Vicki like that, but I was upset about what they might have heard.' He turned abruptly and walked quickly out of the kitchen.

'Can I do anything, Nan?' Judy asked.

'Yes, dear. In about ten minutes bring

them through a cup of cocoa and a biscuit. Yes—and an aspirin for Vicki. She's a very highly strung little girl, and she adores Mark really. It's such a shame.'

Judy thoughtfully tidied the kitchen and did the dishes. What an extraordinary statement to make! She tried to remember Vicki's words. Something about he had to marry Zelda or he would lose all the money. Then Peter mentioned a will. Neither Mark nor Nan had denied that the statement was true. They were both more upset by their own carelessness in leaving the door open. It was easy to understand their dismay at the thought that the children might have learned of the news that their parents were believed dead. And to learn of it in such a manner would have been much worse than if they had been told in a straightforward way. But ' marry Zelda or lose the money ' sounded so extraordinary. Well, it was none of her business.

Judy made up the three cocoa drinks, placed some of the twins' favourite biscuits on a tray, and an aspirin, then carried it through. Nan was sitting on Vicki's bed with her arm around the little girl. Peter was lying on the end of the bed. They were talking quite happily, but Judy noticed that Vicki was still giving an occasional hiccup, and that she had her mother's picture clutched in her hands.

'Oh, how nice, Judy. Come on in. We

were just talking about the twins' mother, Betsy. Let Judy have the photograph while you drink your cocoa, Vicki. Be careful you don't spill it. Cocoa stains are so hard to get out. I am glad you brought me a cup too, Judy.'

Judy looked at the photograph. What a happy family group—Peter and Vicki standing with their parents on the steps of a lovely modern home. The father was tall and dark with a fine intelligent face. The mother had an arm around each twin and was laughing. Judy was surprised to see that their mother was not much taller than the twins.

'Why, you two are nearly as big as your mother,' she commented.

Peter, scenting criticism, said, 'She's little, but she's tough. Dad wouldn't have taken her with him if she hadn't been strong. She can ride and shoot and ski and swim. She used to go mountaineering before she had us. Dad says he would rather have her with him, if he was in a tight corner, than any man he knows.'

'Oh, I'm sure he would,' Judy agreed hastily. 'I think she looks quite lovely. I didn't mean anything derogatory by saying she was tiny. I'm so tall myself that I envy small dainty girls. They look so much more feminine.'

'You're okay,' Peter said gruffly.

'You should see Mummy when she's going

out with Daddy at night,' Vicki put in eagerly. 'She has beautiful dresses, really gorgeous, and wears earrings and everything. Daddy says she looks like a princess. She smells lovely too.'

Judy felt a sudden surge of anger at the missing Paul and Betsy. How could they go off and leave their children? They must have known the risks involved. When you have children, you should stay and look after them, not go gallivanting all over the place. She knew that Mark and Nan loved them and cared for them, but children need their parents.

'When do you think we'll hear from them Nan? It's ages since we had a letter.'

Judy could see Nan looked strained. 'You've finished your cocoa. Nan, you're looking tired. Why don't you go to bed? I'll read a little to the twins. We have only one chapter left to read.'

Nan kissed each child and giving Judy a grateful glance left the room.

'Promise you'll go to your room, Peter, and you'll settle down as soon as I finish, Vicki?' asked Judy as she found the place in the book.

'Yes,' chorused the twins. As Judy's pleasant voice read on they relaxed and became interested in the story, and forgot their worries. When she finished she settled them for the night and went along to see Nan.

'Are they better now?' Nan asked anxiously.

'Yes, right as rain. Don't worry, Nan. You know how children say things they don't mean when they're upset, but they forget quickly. How are you feeling?'

'Better now, thanks. It's so silly to get upset, I know, but when you're under a strain it isn't easy to remain calm. I've taken one of my pills, so I should have a good night.'

'Is there anything I can get you before I go to bed?'

'No, nothing, thanks, dear,' answered Nan. 'Goodnight, Judy, and thanks.'

Judy went out to the kitchen to make sure the fireguard was up and then went to bed. There was no sign of Mark, but she heard him in talking to Vicki and then Peter.

During the night a noise woke Judy. She heard someone moving around in the kitchen. Quickly putting on her brunch coat and slippers, she hurried out in case Nan had taken a bad turn.

'Oh, it's you, Mark. I thought Nan might be not feeling well.'

'Judy, I'm sorry, I was just making some coffee. Did I wake you up?'

'What on earth is the time?' asked Judy, rubbing her eyes.

'About one o'clock. I was busy doing my paper work. I've just finished. Seeing I've woken you up, would you like a cup of coffee?'

Judy walked over and stirred the fire. 'By the look of the table you've had quite a bit to do.'

Mark collected his papers and tidied them up. He poured Judy a cup of coffee and brought it over to her, then sat down opposite her.

'You understate the case. I've had a monumental task. I hate doing my sums. They always tell such a disastrous story. I keep putting it off. I usually pick a wet day, you know: dismal day—dismal task; but I didn't feel like bed tonight, so I thought I'd do a bit on the budget.'

'Well, did you balance it?'

'You have to be joking!' Mark laughed without mirth. 'However, I have a few more months left. To be exact, four, November, December, January and February. Not long considering the state of my books at the moment. But believe me, Judy, I'm going to have this farm. I've sweated my guts out here for five years, I'm not going to lose it.'

Judy sipped her coffee. There didn't really seem anything to say. She knew so little of the situation. Mark lit a cigarette and stretched his long legs out in front of the fire. 'The set-up here is a bit difficult. My uncle had a peculiar sense of humour. He left me the farm provided I could double the production in five years. Then he added quite a few strings. He socked me with a high rent, stipulated of course that I was not to borrow and then threw in a delightful saver. I'm not boring you?'

'Not at all. What was the saver?'

'Oh, really very cute. His old friend Duke Morrison has a lovely daughter Zelda, and Uncle Jack thought he would play Cupid. If I marry Zelda before first of March I'll get ten thousand dollars. This, I may add, I am allowed to use to balance the budget and so gain the farm. The old reprobate!'

Judy's eyes were enormous. 'That was an awful thing to do.'

'Oh, I don't know.' Mark's expression was enigmatic. 'He never married and was always on at me not to leave it until too late. He thought Paul was fortunate marrying young and having a family. This was his way of making his point.'

'What is Zelda like? Do you love her?'

'She's a very nice girl. When she's at home we go around a lot together. I've known her for years.'

'Does she know about the will?'

'Of course not. Only the lawyer, Nan, and myself and Paul know the contents of the will. Oh, I forgot to mention the twins.'

'Would she marry you?'

'I think she might.'

'But what would she think if she found out

that you'd only married her to get the farm?'
Judy was horrified.

'I didn't say that was the only reason I
would have for marrying her. Anyway, she's
a very sensible girl. I'm sure she would think
it a good idea.'

'Sensible? I think it's shocking! However, it's none of my affair.' Judy stood up
and put her cup on the table. 'It beats me
why you bother working so hard or trying to
balance your budget when you've got the
problem already solved.'

'Why are you so angry, Judy?—not that
it doesn't suit you to look angry. I think I've
mentioned it before.'

'I'm not angry, just disgusted. I didn't
think you were like that.'

'Like what?' He was laughing at her.

'Miserable, calculating, someone who would
marry for money. I hope you have all the
happiness you deserve, but I'm sorry for the
girl. Good night!'

'Judy, you're always jumping to conclu-
sions. I never said I was going to marry her.
I was just telling you the terms of the will.'

'I'm not interested.' Judy would have
liked to slam the door, but was scared of
waking the whole household.

Judy was so angry she thumped the pillow
with rage, and then burst into tears. After a
while she stopped and tried to work out why

she was so angry. It wasn't because Mark was going to marry Zelda. If he had said he was in love with Zelda she would have accepted that, but he had implied that it would be a sort of arranged marriage.

He was just despicable. How could she have been so mistaken in his character? She had admired him so much. He was so good with Vicki and Peter. He and his mother shared a wonderful relationship. He worked so hard and was so cheerful—so kind. She had liked him, more than liked him—not loved, that would have been stupid.

I hate him, she told herself firmly. He's just not worth thinking about. I can't leave here because I've found out what he really is. I love Nan and the children. It wouldn't be fair to leave them in the lurch. I will wait until after Christmas. They should have some definite word about the twins' parents by then. And she had to admit it—she wanted to see Zelda. What could she be like? Sensible! Ugh!

Judy fell into an uneasy sleep just before dawn. She didn't wake at the usual time and Nan was surprised to see her come into the kitchen.

'Oh, I thought you were over at the shed, Judy. Didn't you sleep well?' Nan's voice was sympathetic.

'Not very,' admitted Judy. 'I don't think I'll go to the shed this morning. I'll do the lunches, and then start the washing. Do you think it will keep fine? It looks a bit cloudy.'

'The weather report is for rain. We might be lucky. We can always finish the clothes off in the drier if it does rain.'

When Mark and the children came in laughing together, Judy decided grimly that Mark wouldn't get around her as easily as he did the twins.

'Why weren't you at the shed, Judy?' Vicki demanded. 'Were you sick?'

'No, darling, I wasn't sick. Now eat your breakfast or you'll be late for the bus.'

'Oh, I think your prize Judy is just a oncer, kids. You won't see her back in the shed.'

Both twins defended Judy loyally. Peter wasn't having his star pupil maligned or criticized. 'You will come over tonight, won't you, Judy?'

'Of course. Really, you must hurry. Get your cases.' She refused to look at Mark. Drat the man! She had intended keeping as far away from him as possible. Now to pacify the twins she would have to spend a couple of hours a day in his company. After the twins left Judy cleaned the table and stacked the dishes.

'Will you come and give me a hand to move the sheep, Judy?'

'No, I'll be busy in the house today,' she replied brusquely.

'Oh, don't tell me you're still mad at me.'

Mark put a friendly hand on her arm.

'Don't touch me!' Judy flared, shrugging away.

'Temper, temper!'

'What's the matter with you two?' asked Mrs Palmer. 'Have you been teasing her, Mark?'

'No, Nan my pet, I haven't been teasing her. She's disillusioned. She has discovered that I have feet of clay, and is very angry with me.'

'You do flatter yourself, my son. Only finding that their idols have feet of clay upsets people, and I'm sure Judy is much too intelligent to have ever thought you perfect.'

'But you think I'm perfect, don't you, Nan?' queried Mark in a plaintive tone.

'I do not,' replied Nan severely. 'I think you can be most aggravating sometimes. Now get off to work and leave Judy and me in peace.'

'Right, I'm off. Who would want to stay in a house with two bad-tempered women? 'Bye!'

Judy worked furiously. She pegged out the washing, then scrubbed the kitchen, wash-house and verandah. Then she polished the kitchen floor. She tidied and luxed the bedrooms, cleaned the bath and basin, moving like a whirlwind.

Nan called, 'Judy, stop work this minute! Come and have a cup of tea. It's poured out.

Come on, now, the house is as clean as a new pin.'

Judy came through to the kitchen reluctantly. She took her cup of tea but did not drink it. She was ashamed of her bad temper. She knew that she was being unreasonable. Mark meant nothing to her. The very fact that she was being illogical made her even more angry.

Nan's quiet voice interrupted her thoughts. 'What's worrying you, Judy? Can I help? Have you and Mark really quarrelled? Are you angry at him for upsetting the twins last night? Is that it?'

'No, of course not. It's nothing to do with Peter and Vicki. Really, it's nothing at all. I'm just being silly,' Judy said unhappily.

'We're all silly sometimes.' Nan's voice was sympathetic. 'Tell me what it is. I'm fond of you, Judy. I don't like to see you upset.'

'Mark told me about his uncle's will last night, and that to make sure of getting the farm he'll have to marry a girl named Zelda. I thought Mark was such a wonderful person, and now I think he's despicable. To marry a girl for money . . . !' Judy pushed her cup away and walked over to the window, fiercely fighting back the threatening tears. What was the matter with her? She rarely cried, but now she was becoming a real cry-baby.

She stared out of the window until she had control of herself, then realized that Mrs Palmer had not answered her. She turned. 'Don't you think that's terrible, Nan? To marry a girl to get money. Not because he loves her, but because it would be a satisfactory arrangement.'

'Did he tell you that he didn't love her?' questioned Nan.

'No. I asked him if he did, but he didn't say yes or no.'

'Did he definitely say he was going to marry her?' Nan persisted.

'Well, not a definite statement,' Judy spoke as if the words hurt her, 'but his intentions are quite obvious. First he said he couldn't balance his budget, then he said he wasn't going to lose the farm, then he said if he married Zelda Morrison before the first of March everything would be all right.'

Mrs Palmer sighed. 'Well, Mark and Zelda have been friends for years. It's quite on the cards that they will marry. But I can tell you one thing for certain, he won't marry her unless he loves her. Mark talks a lot of nonsense at times, but he has often said to me that unless he's as lucky as Paul in finding a real mate he would never marry. So you can be assured that if they do marry it won't be just for the sake of the farm. Does that make you feel any better?'

'Yes, yes, it does. If it's true,' said Judy

doubtfully. ' It was the thought of him being so calculating, so coldblooded, that upset me. It didn't seem in character. It shocked me. Why do you think he misled me like that?'

' Perhaps to get your reaction?'

' Oh, he got that all right,' said Judy, and laughed.

' That's better, you're smiling again. He was probably only teasing you—or maybe he had some other reason.'

' Nan,' Judy hesitated for a moment, then continued, ' I want to ask you something. How do you know for sure when you are in love? Is there any test? Let me tell you about Bruce. I would like to ask your advice.'

Mrs Palmer listened carefully. Judy told her the whole story from the time she had met Bruce in England until she had given him back his ring.

' Honestly, Nan, he was a completely different person in his own home. In England he was wonderful, lighthearted and full of fun, but once he was with his mother . . .' Judy shrugged her shoulders hopelessly.

' Thank you for telling me, Judy. Mark did tell me, when you first came, that you were only here until you sorted out a personal problem. Have you come to any decision yet?'

' No. That's what's so awful. I've been here nearly two months and I'm still undecided. Bruce is becoming impatient, and I can't blame him really. I've been wanting to talk it over with you. I want to ask you what I should do. Should I marry Bruce?'

Nan looked into Judy's trusting eyes. 'My dear, I wouldn't dream of telling you what you should do. It must be your own decision. It is your life. But I will say this, if you have any doubts, any doubts at all, don't marry him. You must be absolutely sure that he's the right man before you commit yourself.'

'But how can I be sure? Judy cried. 'How did you know that Mark's father was the right man for you? Were you really sure before you married him?'

Nan's smile was sweet. 'Quite, quite sure. When he told me he loved me I felt I was walking on air. When he held my hand I felt safe. His presence gave me comfort, courage, and a sense of belonging. When he kissed me I knew I could never love anyone else. Whether he made me happy or miserable didn't seem important, just so long as I could be with him. Perhaps I was one of the lucky ones, because I knew from the day I met him that he was the only man in the world for me.'

'I don't feel like that about Bruce,' Judy said sadly. 'Yet I like him very much. It seems so unfair to keep him waiting.'

'It would be much more unfair to marry him before you were sure. Take your time, perhaps something will happen to point the way for you.'

It started to rain later in the afternoon and Judy had to race out to the line to rescue the washing.

'Wasn't I lucky? They're all beautifully dry,' she said as she placed the basket on the table.

It rained steadily all the night and the next morning it became heavier. While they were milking, the noise of the rain pelting on the shed roof drowned out the sound of the radio and milking machines. Thunder rolled ominously in the distance. As they finished the storm moved closer and the sky lit up with vivid flashes of lightning. As the thunder crashed overhead the ground actually trembled. Judy was soaked to the skin by the time she reached the house, and was glad to change into dry clothes.

'I've never seen anything like it, Nan. It scares me, yet it's exciting,' remarked Judy as she sat down to breakfast. 'Does it always rain like this? Look at the windows. They're like fish shop windows in town. The water is just bucketing down.'

'I wish we didn't have to go to school,' moaned Peter. 'We'll miss all the flood. The kids on the other bus are lucky. They usually get sent home early when it floods.'

'Do you like floods?' asked Judy, turning to help Vicki button her coat.

'Yes,' said Vicki, her eyes sparkling. 'Last

time we had a raft out on the lawn. It was great fun. Oh, I do hope it comes up properly.'

'You little horrors! What about all the sheep and cattle?' Judy scolded, but the twins did not stop to answer as they ran for the bus.

'Where's Mark, Nan? Isn't he having any breakfast? Whoo! that was close,' Judy cried as the lightning flashed, making the telephone ring.

'He went down to check on the river. I don't think it will be up yet, but it won't be long if this deluge keeps up.'

'How long does it have to rain before it floods?'

'It depends on how heavy the rain is. Rain like this will bring a flood in about five hours. Sometimes it can rain for weeks without flooding.'

'I think that's Mark on the porch now,' said Judy, getting up to put the kettle on. She put his bacon and eggs in the pan and made some toast.

As Mark sat down to the table he looked worried. 'It's going to be a real old man flood. The paddocks are covered with surface water now. I reckon we've had nearly an inch of rain this morning. The thunderstorm is travelling to the north. I'll start moving the stock as soon as I've had this.'

'Can I help?' offered Judy hesitantly.

Mark grinned, 'Decided to forgive me, love?'

'There's nothing to forgive,' Judy replied stiffly.

'Let's say you don't think I'm such a bad bloke after all?' His eyes were amused.

'I'll reserve judgement,' answered Judy.

'You're a hard woman,' Mark laughed. 'I don't think you'd better come with me. It's raining cats and dogs out there. I can manage. There's no need for you to get wet.'

'But I would like to help.' Judy persisted. 'It's not cold rain. I've been wet before. I won't melt.'

'Please yourself, but don't say I didn't warn you.'

Just then the phone rang. Mark answered it and came back. 'Well, if I had any doubts, they're gone. That was Jim—he says it's been raining in the back country all night and the river there has burst its banks. We've got about two hours at the outside.'

All morning Judy helped him bring the sheep, the cattle and the calves up on to the road. The stock were stubborn and hard to move. Judy was appalled at the sight of the Grey River in full flood. It was terrifying to see the ugly brown water surging and boiling past. It was two miles wide from bank to bank and Judy saw huge trees being washed down, some of them being hurled end over end in the raging torrent. She saw some cattle being swept down, far out from the bank. It made her sick to watch their feeble efforts against the tremendous current.

'Some of them will manage to get ashore further down where the river takes a big swing just before the gorge,' Mark told her. 'I've heard that the police stand on the Grey River bridge at Greymouth and put a bullet into the ones that get that far. At least it puts them out of their misery before they get swept over the bar and out to sea. I don't know if it's true or not. I've always been too busy saving my own stock to worry much about anyone else when the flood is on.'

As they mustered the last lot of stray sheep and drove them over to the road, they found that the water had risen alarmingly. It covered the bridge and about a chain each side. The sheep would not face it.

Mark and Judy pushed and shoved and yelled, the dogs barked, but still the sheep would not move.

'We haven't got much time. In five minutes it'll be too late. Push your way through to the front, Judy!' Mark yelled. 'Then lead them in. I'll stay here with the dogs and keep them bunched.'

Judy struggled through the flock of wet, bewildered sheep, and waded into the water. It was well over her gumboots, but by now she was so wet it didn't bother her. Miraculously the sheep followed her and were soon safe on the high ground.

'That's great,' said Mark as he splashed through the water. 'To think I was going to leave you at home! I would have lost that bunch if you hadn't been here. Well, I think we've got the lot. Let's go home and get something to eat. That was close, you know. The river is coming up much more quickly than I expected. I wouldn't have managed without your help. You're a great girl.' He put his arm around her and gave her a hug. 'You poor little thing! You look like a drowned rat.'

'I've had more attractive compliments in my time.' But she smiled as she said it.

To Judy's amazement, Koromiko Creek, the little creek by the house, was a raging river. It had overflowed its banks and the water was flowing all over the lawns, the paths and the gardens.

'Oh, poor Mac! Look at his garden. What a shame! Will it come into the house, Mark?' she asked apprehensively as she rescued some of the twins' toys that were bobbing about in the water.

'No, it's never been through the house to my knowledge. It pours through the washhouse but stops an inch short of the top step. Whoever built this place put it on high piles, but I wouldn't mind if they had put it up another foot. An inch to spare doesn't give you a real feeling of security, does it?'

Nan was delighted to see them home and learn that all the stock was safe. She bustled about putting a hot meal on the table while they changed into dry clothes.

'Won't the dairy cows be in danger, Mark?' asked Judy as she drank her second cup of tea.

'They should be safe for a while. I'll milk early this afternoon in case the power goes off. Then I'll bring them out on the road for the night. There's no use upsetting them too early, and they are pretty safe in that paddock.'

'It wasn't safe enough once,' Nan reminded him.

'Oh, that was years ago.' He explained to Judy, 'The chap who owned the farm then left the cows in that paddock while he came home for a cup of tea. Poor beggar! A wall of water came down the valley and picked up the cows and left them stuck in those big old black pine trees in the bottom paddock. Those trees are about a hundred foot high and half a mile from here, so you can imagine the force of the water. They say the County trucks were carting them out of here for days.'

'How terrible,' cried Judy. 'How can you sit here calmly drinking your tea when the same thing may happen to your herd?'

'Don't worry. I wouldn't be here if I thought there was any risk. That time the embankment about six miles above us gave way. It won't happen again.'

It rained incessantly all afternoon. Mark was out all the time, but he would not let Judy go with him. Judy, heard the milking machine start about half past three and she waded across to the shed. At one part she had to climb along the calf yard rails, because the water between the house and the shed was three or four feet deep with a strong current.

Mark looked up when she came in. 'Why didn't you stay at home? There's no need for you to be out in this mess.'

'I'll stay and help. I'm wet through now, there's no point in going home again.'

As they finished the twins came splashing in. 'Isn't it fun, Judy?' cried Vicki joyfully.

'I'm not sure if you'd call it fun,' smiled Judy.

They all helped to drive the cows through the flood to a special yard behind the house. The rain stopped suddenly, and within half an hour the sky was blue and the sun shining. The twins played happily on the lawn until dark.

'Well, it's all over now,' Judy remarked as they sat by the fire after dinner.

'Not quite,' Mark told her. 'The water is still rising, at least it was the last time I was down the road.'

About ten o'clock when Mark went for a

last look at the stock Judy went with him. He had a series of gates dividing off each lot of animals. Judy found the sight of the flood eerie. The still black water covered the whole farm. Here and there a patch of bush or the top of a fence showed, but the most uncanny part was the light. It was as bright as day. The huge moon reflected on the flood waters and the stars were out in all their glory.

'It's dropping,' Mark said with satisfaction. 'By morning there won't be a sign of water. But there will be a sign left by the flood, most of my fences will be flattened. Home to bed, Judy, we'll worry about that in the morning. The main thing is that I didn't lose any stock.'

CHAPTER VI

On Monday Judy received a letter from Bruce. He had arranged his transfer to Wellington and was leaving Christchurch in three weeks. He wanted to come and see her. In his letter he poured out his love for her, and as Judy read it she felt guilty that it did not awake any response in her own heart. She felt detached, as if she was reading a letter meant for someone else.

Perhaps when she saw him it would be different. Bruce had suggested that he came next Sunday if it suited Judy. He would arrive about ten o'clock. She asked Nan if it would be all right for her to take the day off.

'Of course, Judy. Pack a picnic lunch and get Bruce to take you out to Lake Moana for the day. It's not far and is a really lovely spot. You're quite welcome to have Bruce here to lunch, of course, but I'm sure you would rather be on your own.'

'Oh, that's a lovely idea,' replied Judy gratefully.

All the week she was irritable, absent-minded, and unsettled. She was disgusted with herself because the thought of his visit did not thrill her. She only felt the pleasure she would feel at seeing any acquaintance. She tried to recall him to mind, but he seemed a nebulous figure, indistinct and vague. She gazed at his photograph, but it did not help to bring him to life. She could not marry him feeling the way she did, but the thought of hurting him made her so very unhappy. He loved her so much, and once she had loved him. It seemed so cruel to dash his hopes for the second time.

For hours she brooded and worried and came no nearer to finding the answer. She liked him, better than any man she had ever met. Mark? Angrily she tried to erase that thought from her mind. Mark was going to marry Zelda. She must come to a decision. The uncertainty was wearing her down.

On Saturday morning Peter rushed into the kitchen. 'Judy, Uncle Mark is going to the islands to get a load of sand. Will you come with us?'

'No, but thanks for asking me.'

Mark and Vicki came in as she refused Peter. Vicki, always direct and to the point, cried angrily, 'You've been crabby all week. You won't go anywhere with us. We wanted you to help us birdnesting last night, and you wouldn't. It's frightfully important to Peter. You just don't care. Don't you like living here any more?'

Judy saw their angry disappointed faces, and was instantly repentant. 'Of course I do, Vicki. I'm sorry I've been crabby.'

'Then you'll come?' urged Peter. 'It's a corker place. We have to go across the creek, and up through the bush. Then we cross a few streams of the river on to the island. It's the only place Uncle Mark can get good cementing sand. I have to get some birds' eggs for my project. We'll find a lot there.'

'Do come,' said Vicki, sensing that Judy was weakening. 'I want to find some stones. Teacher said if we bring him some pretty ones he'll put them in his tumbler and polish them for us. You can make them into lovely brooches or pendants. I want to get a special one for Mummy for Christmas.'

'Leave Judy alone, you brats. She has a lot on her mind. She doesn't want to be bothered by your chatter today. If you're coming with me you'd better look slippy,' said Mark as he walked out.

The twins stood silently pleading. Suddenly Judy made up her mind. 'I'll go. Run out and tell Mark to wait a minute.'

Mrs Palmer encouraged Judy: 'Good girl! You'll enjoy yourself. The fresh air will do you good. You've been looking quite pale this week.'

'But the work? I'm going to be away ...'

'Bother the work,' replied Nan. 'You've hung the washing out and done the rooms. I'll be glad to have the house to myself, old ladies need peace and quiet.'

'Old ladies, poof! You know you're not much older than Vicki at heart,' laughed Judy. 'In fact compared to you, I sometimes feel positively ancient. However, thanks for your blessing. I'd better hurry or Mark will drive off and leave me.'

Judy scrambled on to the trailer with the twins. She was going to forget her problems today and have fun. The ground was rough and they were bounced around on the trailer. The twins growled about Mark's driving and giggled happily. It was a beautiful day, warm and sunny. They drove down the farm lane which was lined with hawthorn trees, in full bloom. They reminded Judy of home in England, but as soon as she lifted her gaze and saw the majestic Southern Alps her memories fled. How grand they were, providing a permanent backdrop of beauty to every view.

Mark drove past the old orchard and crossed the Koromiko Creek, then across some open country to stop by a lagoon bordered by huge kowhai trees and willows. Flax bushes edged the lake, and a flock of wild ducks took wing as Mark stopped the tractor. Judy was spellbound when she heard the clear liquid notes of the mocking bird. Two pigeons flew to another tree with a soft whirr of wings.

'See, Judy, up there, that's a tui—see his white throat. He's sometimes called a parson bird,' Peter pointed out. Suddenly a tiny fantail flew inquisitively nearer. Judy was fascinated.

'Oh, isn't he beautiful? So tame.' She

stretched out her hand to touch it, but it flitted a little further away and continued its erratic dance. Mark started the tractor and drove on.

They travelled through some bush, then out on to a green river bank, forded several small streams and stopped by a huge sandbank.

'Well, off you go while I load up,' said Mark.

The twins needed no second bidding. Judy followed as they ran off. Vicki searched diligently for unusual coloured stones, exclaiming in delight whenever she made a find. Peter hunted for nests, but had no luck as they had been swept away in the recent flood. They found a small clear pool with cock-a-bullies in it and spent a happy time trying to catch them, but the tiny darting fish were too clever at camouflaging themselves.

They heard Mark returning for his second load and hurried back to him. They put their treasures carefully in the tool box. Judy stood admiring the effortless ease with which Mark shovelled the sand. He was stripped to the waist, and deeply tanned. His muscles rippled as he dug, then threw the sand on to the trailer. How fit and active he was!

'Come on, Judy,' called Peter. 'We'll go over to the big trees on the river bank. We're sure to find some nests there. Can we, Uncle Mark?'

'Sure, go ahead, but don't go too far away from the track. I'll be leaving in about twenty minutes and I'm in a hurry.'

Judy and the twins were quickly on the river bank searching for birds' nests in the high trees.

'There's one!' shouted Vicki excitedly, pointing upwards. 'No, not there, further out, just above that dead branch.'

'Good. Help me up to the first branch, Judy,' demanded Peter. He climbed fearlessly higher and higher.

'Be careful, Peter, do be careful,' called Judy anxiously. 'That branch doesn't look very safe.'

'I can't reach it, Judy. Do you think you could come up here? You're a lot taller than me. I'm sure you could get it. Oh, do have a go.' He peered down at her.

'You come down first. I don't think I could even get to the first branch,' Judy answered reluctantly.

Peter was down in a flash, and examined the situation. Then he marshalled his forces like a general in the field. 'It's only the first branch that's difficult, after that it's easy. Now, Vicki and I will kneel down and you stand on our backs. That ought to give you a start.'

'Oh, I couldn't! I might hurt you,' Judy protested.

'You're only skinny, you wouldn't be as

heavy as me. You're not scared, are you?' There was a world of scorn in his voice.

'Of course not,' replied Judy hastily, and stepped gingerly on to their backs, then reached up and grasped the branch.

The twins stood up as soon as they felt her weight off them. 'That's it, Judy,' encouraged Peter. 'Swing your leg over. Yes, like that. Now pull yourself up. Hurry, we haven't got much time. I can hear the tractor.'

Judy panted and heaved, and searched desperately for safe holds as she climbed higher. If she hadn't been so short of breath she would have told Peter a thing or two. Skinny indeed! Little horror!

Now she was opposite the nest and began inching her way out along the dead branch.

'A little bit further, Judy. Just a little bit further. You can do it,' Peter called helpfully.

As she took the nest, she heard the branch crack frighteningly and she began to fall. Twice she nearly saved herself, but each time the branches tore from her hands.

Her head was throbbing violently. Slowly she opened her eyes. Someone was bathing her face with a wet cloth. 'What happened?'

'Oh, Uncle, she's not dead.' Peter's voice was shaky.

'No thanks to you. You limb of Satan, sending her up that tree . . . I'll tan the hide off you when I get home!'

'Judy, we're sorry. Truly!'

That sounded like Vicki. She must sit up.

'Take it easy, Judy. Just rest for a bit. You've had a nasty fall. What in the world possessed you to climb up there?'

'A bird's nest. I wanted to get Peter a bird's nest,' Judy answered, still feeling slightly muzzy.

'My God, you frightened me to death. The twins came screaming out on to the track, yelling that they'd killed you. When I found you, I thought they might be right.' He wiped her face again.

'I'll be fine. I'm sorry to hold you up.'

'Don't be so daft. I'm thankful you didn't break your neck. I don't think you've broken any bones. Next time you go climbing, take a parachute.'

'Help me up, Mark.' He lifted her carefully to her feet and she leaned against him for support. 'I think I have twisted my ankle.' She grimaced with pain. 'I can't put my weight on it.'

'You twins shoot off and make a comfortable place ready on the trailer for Judy. I'll carry her along in a few minutes when she's feeling better.'

He helped her to a fallen log and lifted her up, then took off her sandal. 'Yes, you've broken or sprained your ankle. Is your head better now? I'd like to get you to a doctor as soon as possible.'

'Yes, I'm feeling much better. I was really

lucky, having all those fallen leaves to land on, and the branches broke my fall. I'm ready when you are.' She eased herself down off the log. 'If you give me an arm I could hop along to the trailer.'

'Just one arm? Oh, I think two would be much better.' He put his arms around her and held her close. 'What am I to do with you, Judy? There's your intended coming tomorrow to claim you, and you'll be hobbling round on crutches. You'll have bits of sticking plaster here and there, and if I'm not mistaken, a lovely shiny black eye.'

She looked up at him, intending to make some light remark, but the look in his eyes silenced her. She felt breathless—shaky—it must be the effects of the fall.

Mark said, 'I know it's mean to take advantage of an injured person, but do realize that tomorrow you may well be engaged to be married, and quite out of my reach. You'll just have to forgive me, the temptation is just too strong to resist.'

Slowly his arms tightened and his lips came down on hers. As she surrendered to the sweetness of his kiss, she knew with blinding certainty that she could never marry Bruce. So this was love!

As he drew away she looked into his face. How long she had loved him and not known it? How stupid she had been! Wonderingly she put her hand up to touch his cheek.

'I'm sorry, Judy. I shouldn't have kissed you. Even if you're free, I'm not. I was crazy, a thoughtless fool.' His face was pale under his tan. 'Judy, you're crying! Oh, my dear, forgive me.'

He swung her into his arms, and carried her along the track to where the children were waiting.

'Good kids. You sit this side, Peter,' he said as he lowered Judy on to the trailer. 'That's right, Vicki, you sit here. Don't talk to Judy, let her rest, and I'll drive as carefully as I can.'

As soon as they arrived home Mrs Palmer took charge calmly and efficiently. She soon had Judy in a warm bath and gently washed the bruises and cuts. 'You were very fortunate, Judy, to get off so lightly. Oh, I know you're stiff and sore and scratched, but you could have so easily been seriously injured. Those wretched grandchildren of mine . . . !'

'You won't let Mark punish them, will you, Nan?' Judy interrupted. 'It wasn't their fault.'

'Of course not. He knows how upset they are because you're hurt.' Nan helped her dress, and after lunch Mark drove her into town to the doctor.

Doctor Jones gave her a thorough examination and pronounced her quite sound except for her ankle. 'I'm sending you to hospital for an X-ray. If they find a break they'll put you in plaster. If it's a sprain, they'll strap it up for you. Keep off that foot for the first three days and then use crutches. They'll give you a pair at the hospital.'

He went to the door and called Mark in. 'Right, you can take her away. Bring her back in a week. You, young lady, leave climbing trees to those more suited to it, and then you won't interrupt my weekend again.' But he smiled to take the sting out of his words.

Judy was exhausted by the time they left the hospital. Her foot was neatly strapped and felt more comfortable, but they had had a long wait and she felt so tired. They drove home in silence.

At the gate Mark helped her with her crutches. Judy said, 'I'm sorry you've had to waste all afternoon with me. You won't get any cementing done now.'

'Damn the cementing!' He saw her safely inside and then left abruptly.

Judy sat on the sofa, while the twins took turns trying out her crutches. When Mark called them at milking time Judy asked Mrs Palmer to put a call in to Bruce's number in Christchurch.

Mrs Palmer came back from the telephone. 'There's a twenty-minute delay, Judy. I wish you'd go to bed and have a rest.'

'I want to speak to Bruce first. I'm going to ask him not to come over tomorrow. It's no use, I can't marry him.'

Mrs Palmer looked at Judy anxiously. 'Are you sure, Judy?'

'Quite sure, Nan,' Judy replied, wishing that the phone would ring. Now she had made up her mind she wanted to get the ordeal over. 'Something happened today to show me that I can't marry him.' She lay back on the sofa and closed her eyes, and Mrs Palmer wisely left her in peace.

When the phone shrilled, she felt quite sick as she gathered her crutches and hopped through behind Mrs Palmer.

'It's Bruce, Judy,' said Mrs Palmer, handing her the receiver, and walked out, shutting the door behind her.

Judy explained to Bruce that she had had a fall and was unable to go out with him on Sunday.

'I don't mind, Judy. I want to see you. Surely I can come to the house and visit you?'

So she steeled herself and told him she could not marry him. It was not easy; she hated to hurt him.

'Don't upset yourself, Judy,' Bruce said quietly. 'I was half expecting this. I could tell from your letters that there wasn't much hope for me. I love you, Judy. I think I always will, you're not a girl anyone could forget easily. I realize that I lost you through my own stupidity. There doesn't seem much more to say, except that I hope some day we may meet again as friends. If you ever need me, you have my address. Goodbye, Judy, my darling.'

She heard him hang up and walked through to her room feeling mentally and physically exhausted. Oh, why was life so difficult? Who said that being in love was a wonderful experience—it wasn't, it was painful, it tore you to shreds, it hurt. She crawled into bed, and her pillow was wet with tears before she slept.

She woke up to find Vicki by her bed. 'What's the time, Vicki? Have you finished milking?'

'It's late, we've had dinner ages ago. Nan sent me in to see if you were awake and would like something to eat. You're not to get up. You scared us when you fell out of that tree.' Vicki looked at her reproachfully.

Judy laughed, 'It scared me too, Vicki. What happened to the nest?'

'You squashed it. All the eggs were broken.'

'Oh well, that's life, Vicki,' Judy smiled. 'Tell Nan I would love a cup of tea if it's not too much trouble.'

A few minutes later Nan came in followed by Mark carrying a tray. He put the tray down. 'I'll be back to collect this later.'

'Oh, Nan, I feel terrible giving you this extra work. I'm supposed to be here looking after you, and here I am lying in bed, with you doing all the work. I'm feeling fine now.'

'That's good. Now I'll leave you to have

your dinner. I told Mark you'd rung Bruce. You don't mind?'

'No, not at all. I would rather he knew. It's all over now. It wouldn't have worked out. Thanks for letting me talk to you, Nan. You helped me more than you'll ever know.'

'I'm glad,' answered Nan. She patted Judy's shoulder and went out.

When Judy had eaten the delicious meal she put the tray away and lay back and closed her eyes. This was the first chance she had had to examine the exciting discovery she had made this morning. She loved Mark. Even thinking of him gave her a feeling of excitement. No wonder she had been unable to think seriously about marrying Bruce—she had been unconsciously comparing him with Mark, always to his detriment. She must be careful. Mark must not suspect that his kiss had been the reason for her breaking off with Bruce. It would only embarrass him. He was going to marry Zelda. He had only been flirting with her to pass the time, she knew that. He had been honest with her. Even this morning he had told her he wasn't free.

'You asleep?' It was Mark taking her tray.

Judy opened her eyes. 'No, just thinking.'

'I'd like to talk to you if you're not too tired.'

'Go ahead, I've had a good sleep. You're not going to start growling at me again for climbing trees?'

'No,' Mark replied as he sat down on the end of the bed, taking care not to disturb her foot. 'Nan tells me you're not going to marry Bruce.'

Judy watched him carefully. She wished she knew what he was thinking, and blushed. It was lucky he didn't know what she was thinking. She looked down and started pleating the sheet between her fingers, nervously. 'No. I've thought it over carefully and I don't think we would have been happy together.'

'I'm glad. He wasn't the man for you, too wishy-washy.'

Judy smoothed the sheet out and started pleating it again as if it was her only interest in life. 'What sort of a man do you think I need?'

'Someone to boss you. Bruce would have let you have your own way all the time—very bad for your character. Are you very unhappy?'

'No, just relieved.'

'Good. Now that's settled, let's talk business. You came here to have a place where you could think until you could come to a decision. Now that a decision has been made what are your plans? Will you stay on here a few more months? At least until we get some definite news from abroad. What do you say?'

Judy had been trying to concentrate on his

words, but her thoughts were chaotic. 'Oh, Mark, Mark,' cried her heart, 'I'd stay for ever if you'd ask me.' Had he no idea what effect he was having on her? He was so close she could put her hand out and touch him. He was waiting patiently for her answer.

'I haven't made any plans yet. I want to get back to nursing eventually, but there's no rush. I love Nan, and the children. I know it sounds funny, but I feel closer to Nan than I do to my own mother. I would like to be here when the news comes, just in case it isn't good. They'll need me then.' She looked directly at him.

This time it was Mark who turned away. 'I'm very grateful, Judy. I don't know how to thank you. Will you stay until March? Would you be prepared to stay that long?'

Judy's heart sank. He would not need her after that date because Zelda would be here to take care of Nan and the twins. 'Yes, I'll stay.'

'Will you promise me that no matter what happens you'll stay until the beginning of March? I would like something definite so that I can plan my work.'

'Yes, I give you my word,' Judy answered quietly. How funny listening to him begging her to stay, when that was the only thing in the world she wanted to do. Just to be near him was heaven, but he couldn't know that. How dear he was to her! How could she leave without seeing Zelda? She wouldn't have been human if she did not hope for a miracle. That something might happen?

Three months was quite a long time. Who knows?

CHAPTER VII

Judy enjoyed her three days of enforced rest. She felt relaxed and happy as she sat on the sofa, doing small jobs that normally she had little time for. She sewed buttons on, darned jerseys, and caught up on her correspondence. She had received letters from her mother and father the previous week. As she answered them, she felt a greater affection for her parents than she had felt for years. Who was she to judge them? She had nearly made the same mistake as they had. Her mother had been just eighteen and her father a year older when they had married. As the years passed they had drawn further and further away from each other, they had quarrelled incessantly, and while her mother had loved company, loved parties and outings, her father had been a quiet, bookish person. They had rubbed each other raw. Perhaps they had been wise to part. In fact they were now better friends than they had been when they were married to each other. She realized now that they did love her, that they had always tried to minimize the effect of their divorce on her. It had been she herself who had held aloof, blaming them for her unhappy childhood. With this new understanding, she felt all the bitterness drain away.

At the end of the week the doctor checked her ankle, and advised her to keep off it as much as possible for the next two weeks, otherwise she would have a permanently weak ankle. Mark put a comfortable chair out in the garden, where Judy spent much of her time watching Mac at his work. She had become quite good friends with Mr McTaggart over the past two months. She had come to respect and admire the old man for his wisdom and honest upright standards. He did not talk a lot. Judy had to work hard to extract any information she wanted. She knew that he had been a miner most of his life, and since he retired he had a gold claim which he worked in his spare time. He had promised to take Judy up to see his claim.

Judy hopped out on her crutches to her chair and sat enjoying the warm sunlight and listening to the birds singing. She noted the meticulous care with which Mac transplanted the tiny lettuce plants. She was beginning to feel restless, tied to her chair. The first week she had been as happy as a lark. Her love for Mark had been so new, so precious, she had hoarded it like a hidden treasure, content that she loved him, not worried whether he loved her in return. She loved him, she could see him every day, that was all she asked for then. As the days passed she began to long for some sign that he found her attractive, that he liked her more than as a friend. But there was nothing. He was friendly, teasing, cheerful, and that was all. Since the day she had fallen from the tree and he had kissed her, he had erected an invisible barrier between them.

'Well, lassie, you're improving on those contraptions,' Mac's voice interrupted her thoughts.

'Yes, I am. By the end of this week I should be able to return them to the hospital.'

Mac had finished the transplanting and sat down on the wheelbarrow, beside her. He lit his pipe and puffed away contentedly.

'Were you ever married, Mac?' she asked.

'I was.'

Judy waited patiently. There was no use trying to prompt him, that much she had learnt. If he had something to say he would tell her in his own good time.

'Ah, she was a bonnie lassie. Her hair was the same colour as your own, like fire in the sun. My bonnie Jean, wilful, wayward, loving and kind. She had plenty of spirit, and a heart as big as the whole world. You make me think of her, only her eyes were blue.'

'How long have you been on your own, Mac?' Judy's voice was soft.

'A long time,' he sighed. 'Thirty years, yet sometimes it feels like only yesterday she was by me. She drowned saving a young boy. Two children were swept out to sea in a rip tide. She managed to save one, but perished with the other. She should not have gone back in after the other boy, but it was like her not to count the cost. When they came to tell me, I couldn't believe it at first, that anyone as full of life as she ...' He drew on his pipe. 'Time is a marvellous friend, Judy. Time heals all wounds.'

They sat in silence for a long time, then Judy asked, 'You never thought of marrying again? You must have been a young man when she died.'

'No, never. Who could take my Jeannie's place?'

'Do you believe there's someone special for each person?' Judy persisted.

'Yes, and I found mine,' Mac smiled at Judy, 'and I think you've found yours.'

Judy blushed. 'How do you know?'

'I may not say much, but I see a lot. Mark is a fine man. You've got a good chap.'

Judy burst out, 'That's just the trouble, Mac, I haven't got him. He doesn't love me. He's going to marry Zelda Morrison.'

'Rubbish!'

'It isn't rubbish, he told me so himself—or as good as,' Judy said miserably. 'In three months' time.'

'Is she wearing his ring?'

'No.'

'No, and she never will, if you've got any gumption. Go in and fight for him if you think he's worth it. You have everything on your side, you live in his house, you work with him. In three months, my Jeannie could have moved mountains, and so can you. Think on, what does he want most in the world?'

'To get this farm,' replied Judy.

'Well, help him win it. By the time he has achieved his ambition, it will be you he turns to, mark my words.'

'I wish I had money,' said Judy desolately.

'Don't be so foolish, woman. What can money buy? Can it buy happiness? Can it buy health, or love? Do you think if you had money Mark would take or marry you for it? You don't know your man. He wouldn't want to be beholden to any woman, least of all his wife. Mark wants the satisfaction of beating this on his own. What would he have gained to have it handed to him on a plate?'

'A farm,' said Judy bitterly.

Mac stood up and knocked his pipe out. 'I must get back to work, instead of blathering here all day. When you marry Mark, I will have your wedding ring made from gold I've won from my claim. Now put on that loving smile of yours and remember that no one ever won anything worthwhile without a bit of a struggle.'

Perhaps Mac had something there, Judy thought. It would do no harm to try. She loved Mark enough to want to see him get the farm, whether he married her or not. If she helped him, maybe he would be able to finance it himself, and he would not then need extra money. He would not need to marry Zelda—but what if he loved Zelda?

November passed and then December. Day by day Judy worked beside Mark, always cheerful and willing to help. He gratefully accepted her offer to milk each night, with the twins to assist her. It gave him another two hours to work. And how hard he worked! During the day he ploughed and worked and sowed the paddocks. At night he sheared the sheep. Each afternoon Judy would bring in about fifty sheep and after dinner Mark would shear them. So, slowly, the flock was shorn and the bales filled and railed away. Nan worried and scolded him for working too hard, but it made not one iota of difference; he drove himself to the utmost.

Christmas passed with scarcely a ripple. Mrs Palmer was very worried that the twins would miss their parents badly at Christmas; however, the parcels that their parents had left ready in case they were not back by Christmas seemed to satisfy them. As they opened them and read the cards they were reassured of their parents' love and talked eagerly of their return.

It was school holidays now and they were enjoying themselves immensely, helping with the haymaking, going swimming, and in general keeping everyone on their toes waiting for the next disaster.

Early in January Mark had another letter from the leader of the expedition. He wrote saying there was a rumour that two white people were known to be living with a tribe far in the hinterland. He begged them not to be too hopeful, as it could be two missionaries, or some government officials. However, he felt that he could not leave with a clear conscience unless he checked the rumours out on the offchance that it could be Paul and Betsy. He warned them that the chance was slight and that he would visit them on his return to New Zealand in February.

Mrs Palmer was confident that it would prove to be her son and his wife. Nothing could shake her. 'Oh, I'm glad we have kept all this worry from the twins!'

Mark was not so sure and tried to caution her against a further disappointment. They all watched anxiously for the mail each day.

Judy often went down to the Stillwater tennis club after dinner. She enjoyed a game of tennis and played well. Mark had taken her down and introduced her, and she knew Claire and Steve quite well now. They had been friends since the first night that Claire had played chaperone, and of course Steve was quoted daily by the twins as 'teacher says'. They were enthusiastic members of the club, so Judy saw quite a lot of them.

Mark had told her, 'I won't be able to take you very often, but you can take the car whenever you wish.'

Judy often went home with Claire for coffee after a game. One evening after she had helped Claire put the children to bed and Steve had gone back to school to work they sat chatting.

'What is Zelda Morrison like, Claire? I often hear her name mentioned at the club and I gather she's Mark's girl-friend. Where is she, anyhow?' Judy sounded deliberately casual.

'Oh, Zelda? She's a nice kid—sort of small and blonde and sweet. You'll like her, everyone does. Yes, she and Mark have always been close. Her father was a domineering old pig, and I think she used to head for Mark whenever the going got rough. He would set her on her feet and give her the necessary courage to stand up to her old man. I don't know if they're any more than good friends, but you never can tell.'

'No, you can't,' answered Judy lightly. 'Where is she now?'

'In Australia. She's very artistic, and won some sort of designing competition. Look, I'm not really sure of my facts, but one thing I do know, she's coming home at the beginning of February. I heard her cousin say so the other day.'

Mark sold his wool in the January wool

sale. The price of wool had slumped badly at the Wellington and Auckland sales, and dropped again disastrously at Christchurch. Mark's wool cheque was six hundred dollars less than he had allowed for in his budget. His face was set and stubborn after he had spent a night working on his accounts. The next morning he said, 'Right, Nan, there's no other way out, I'll have to make up the deficiency by cutting flax. Provided I really go at it, I can make six hundred dollars by March. I get nine dollars a ton here at the gate—say sixty tons, I can do it.'

'I hate you starting that, Mark. It's such heavy work—not so much the cutting but the carrying out. I'm always scared you'll cut yourself, or tip the tractor up. The ground is so rough up there. Isn't there any other way?'

'Cattle prices are good at the moment, but they could drop. I can't afford to count on them to adjust the balance. I have to keep the stock numbers up anyhow.' He turned to Judy. 'Do you mind keeping on with the evening milking? If it's too much for you tell me. I don't want to kill you with work.'

Judy noted the new lines of strain around Mark's eyes and answered unhesitantly, 'It's no trouble, Mark. I love the work, and the twins are a great help.'

So each morning after milking, wet or fine, Mark set off with his lunch to cut flax. He sometimes took a morning off for stock work, but never any time for relaxation or pleasure.

Judy went up with him occasionally, and sat and watched as he swung the sharp sickle-shaped knife in a steady rhythmical movement, slicing through the flax just above the roots. He tied each bundle of flax with a special knot at each end—twenty-four bundles to the ton. Working steadily all day with only a short break for lunch, Mark could cut three tons a day. He then had to carry them over rough country to the trailer and bring them home, and the flax-mill lorry picked it up at the gate.

Judy marvelled at the terrific pace he worked, never stopping, never flagging. One day she stayed to share his lunch.

'Why are you killing yourself like this, Mark? Surely there's no need to work so hard. You said you're going to marry Zelda and then you'll get the farm. What's the point of this effort?'

Mark grinned his old wicked teasing grin, that she saw so rarely these days. 'You would rather I didn't work? You think I should sit back and wait for Zelda to come home?'

'No,' Judy stammered.

'Wouldn't it be a shocker if she turned me down? I've just got to cover all bets.'

'But you are going to marry her?' Judy persisted, in spite of the ache in her heart she had to know.

'I want to make this on my own, Judy, it's

136

something I have to do. When or if I'm successful, I'll marry the girl I love.'

'So you think love is important?'

'Perhaps. Now off you go home. I'm not wasting my time talking when I could be working. Go away, you're distracting me.'

'I wish I could distract you,' she muttered under her breath as she walked away.

She had followed Mac's advice to the letter, and where had it got her? Nowhere. Mark was friendly, and deeply grateful for her help. He teased her, growled at her, laughed at her, but really he treated her no differently from the way he treated Vicki. Well, Judy decided, she was no child. She would show him. She was sick of playing little-goody-two-shoes; not that she minded helping him, but romancewise it was not getting her anywhere. Zelda would be home soon, and her chance would be gone. What he needed was a good shock, someone else on the scene, perhaps? Come to think of it, the last time he had kissed her was when Bruce was due for the day. Since that day he had kept his distance, behaved so very, very brotherly. Well, bother it, she did not need a brother!

When she came to Koromiko Creek, she sat down on the bank to think out some plan. Competition, that was the answer—but who? Her eyes gleamed as she cast her mind over the available material. There were not many eligible men about. Most of the male visitors to the farm were married. The young student teacher who boarded with Claire and Steve? No, he was too young. One by one she discarded the prospective males from her list. The vet?—now he was really something, quite a dish. Unfortunately he had recently become engaged. She had no intention of hurting anyone by her schemes, yet it had to be a man who would make Mark sit up and take notice. She had to find out if he had any feeling for her at all. If he ignored the fact that she was going out with someone else, then she would know that he didn't care. She had to find out.

Suddenly she laughed out loud. Right under her nose all the time, and she had missed him! The herd-tester, who was due any day now. He usually arrived about two in the afternoon, took samples at the evening milking, stayed the night and left after lunch the following day. Lucky Costelle was a strange man. Mark seemed to get on with him quite well, but Judy noticed none of the other farmers had a good word to say for him. He had apparently built up a fairly shocking reputation as far as women were concerned. When she had asked Mark if the stories were true he had laughed and said, 'Oh, I don't think he's as bad as they make out. He told me once that he considered himself as God's gift to the farmers' wives. He brightened the lives of the lonely ones and he said the farmers were always much nicer to their wives when he was around—just in case. You keep out of the shed when he's here, after all, there's no smoke without fire.'

She had been looking forward to meeting him, expecting to see someone looking as handsome as a Greek god, but Lucky wasn't handsome, in fact his thin angular face had just missed being ugly. It was his eyes that fascinated Judy—deep brown, almost black —and hard, as if they had looked on this world and found nothing good. He was over thirty, and moved with the grace of a panther. He made Judy feel rather uneasy at first. He was cynical and sarcastic and yet there was something appealing about him, a little-boy-lost look. She thought that must be what attracted the women to him.

He treated Mrs Palmer with graciousness and charm, and he was always extremely polite to Judy, but the twins he adored. They thought he was utterly wonderful, and hardly left his side from the time he arrived until he left. Judy thought of the way Claire had described him, 'a lean and hungry man, with magnetism you could almost touch, a danger to any female between eight and eighty.' Hmm—well, Judy did not intend to become one of his conquests, but if she went out with him she was sure Mark would have something to say, and after all that was the object of the exercise.

Judy stood up and waded through the creek, breaking off a sprig of koromiko tree. She admired the small clusters of pale-lilac-to-white flowers, and carried it home with her. Mrs Palmer was talking to Mac in the garden, when Judy joined them.

'You're up to something wicked, lassie. Come on, out with it!' Mac demanded.

'How can you tell?' Judy wanted to know.

'My Jeannie used to get the very same look in her eye when she was bent on mischief. Are you going to let us into the secret?'

'No, I'm not. It wouldn't be a secret any more then, but I'll make you both a cup of tea,' and she ran gaily inside. Nan liked Lucky, so he couldn't be that bad, although Mark always said Nan would make excuses for the Devil himself. Nan had told Judy that Lucky was either separated from his wife or divorced, she was not sure, but she knew there were children involved.

Shortly after Lucky arrived on the following Saturday, it seemed as if Fate was playing into Judy's hands. The telephone rang while they were having afternoon tea, and it was for Lucky. As he left the room Judy thought again how gracefully he moved, like a cat stalking its prey. Maybe she was mad to think of trying to use him.

As he returned to the table he said, 'Well, I've suffered a grievous disappointment. The lady who was to accompany me to the cabaret tonight has been forced to forgo the pleasure of my company. Her husband has returned home—so disobliging of him, don't you think? It does seem a shame to waste these tickets. Perhaps you could use them, Mark? Give Judy a night out?'

Judy held her breath. Silently she begged him to take them.

'No, thanks all the same, Lucky, I think I'll have an early night. I'm sure you won't have any difficulty getting another partner.'

Judy was sick with disappointment. Serve him right if he did get upset when she went out with Lucky! she thought viciously. Well, that was provided Lucky would take her. She had to wait until she could get Lucky on his own. When Mark sent the twins for the cows, and went himself to set up the shed, Judy followed Lucky out to the front gate where he had parked his van.

As he was about to get in Judy called, 'Wait a minute, Lucky, I want to talk to you, please.'

He stopped and leaned back against the van. His stillness frightened Judy, and her courage nearly failed. He made her feel so young and immature. He was waiting, she could not back out now. 'If you haven't anyone to take to the cabaret, would you take me?'

He raised his eyebrows, and Judy felt a crimson tide of colour sweep her face. 'Why?'

His voice was as soft as velvet.

'I never go out anywhere. I thought I'd like a night out.'

'Not true. Tell me your real reason.'

Judy turned away for a moment. She would have to tell him the truth or he would not take her. She took a deep breath. 'Because I want to make Mark jealous.'

Lucky half closed his eyes and smiled. 'Your Mark is a formidable rival. What happens to me if you're successful?'

Judy gave him a steady look. 'You're not scared of any man.'

'True, but also I'm not a fool. You're in love with Mark?'

'Yes.'

'And he's not—how shall I put it delicately —not coming up to scratch?'

'No, he's not,' admitted Judy. 'He says he's going to marry another girl.'

'You don't easily accept defeat. I like that, we shall get on well together. You have unsuspected depths, my dear. Fancy me writing you off as a sweet young thing. Perhaps you have possibilities? What's in this for me?'

'Nothing,' Judy answered flatly.

'You know my reputation?'

'Yes,' Judy answered without faltering.

'You have courage but no intelligence. Mark is a man who will brook no competition. He won't share you, I warn you.'

'He's not being asked to share me. I'm his

if he wants me. At the moment I can't find out if he cares for me or not. If he blows a fuse because I go out with you, then I'll know that there's some hope.'

'My motto, young Judy, is, "I shall do nothing for nothing." You may not get out of this as lightly as you imagine,' Lucky smiled cynically.

'I'm not scared of you.' Which is a whopping lie! thought Judy, crossing her fingers.

'You think I go around like Cupid patching up unhappy romances? You insult me.'

'I think I'll be quite safe with you,' Judy replied quietly.

'That's an even bigger insult. I'll take you to the cabaret, if that's what you want. You'll enjoy yourself. If Mark hangs one on me we'll then know we've been successful, huh?' His smile had genuine humour in it this time. 'Be ready at seven. We'll have dinner in town. This van is my only means of transport. You don't think it too humble a conveyance to take a lady on such a dangerous mission?'

Judy laughed, 'I'll be honoured to ride in your van.'

As Lucky slipped into the truck and slammed the door, she stepped forward. 'Thank you very much for being so nice.'

Lucky growled, 'If this gets out it'll ruin my reputation. We shall have to select some very public spot, and you can slap my face so that people will know I'm not losing my touch!' He waved and drove off.

Judy felt her spirits lift. Lucky was nice, it was going to be fun. She danced along the path and into the kitchen. She smiled to herself as she helped Nan prepare the dinner.

'You're looking very pleased with yourself, Judy,' said Nan with an inquiring glance.

'Oh, I am, Nan. Lucky is taking me to the cabaret, and we're having dinner in town.'

'Splendid. I hope you have a lovely evening,' Nan smiled.

'You do like Lucky, don't you, Nan?'

'Yes, I do. He's so gentle and kind with the children, they bring out the best in him. He has been very badly hurt at one time. It's very easy to preach when you've never met real trouble. He's very bitter, but life hasn't been kind to him.'

'You don't think I'm stupid to go out with him?' Judy asked anxiously.

'Not at all. I think an evening out with Lucky would be a very exciting and memorable experience. Now run along, dear, and make yourself pretty, while I do the dinner.'

Judy bathed luxuriously, after adding her most wickedly expensive bath salts with a generous hand. It was fortunate that she had washed her hair that morning, so she brushed it until it shone, and was glad that she had decided to grow it long. Usually she wore it loose, or in a ponytail to keep it tidy, but tonight she swept it high on her head giving her an elegant sophisticated look. She did her nails with care, and spent a considerable time on her make-up.

Tonight Mark was going to see a very different Judy. Gone were her shirts and trews, gone were her fresh little cotton frocks, and in their place she chose from her wardrobe her most glamorous full-length evening frock. As it fell in soft folds to her feet, she smoothed it gently into place. When she had been nursing in England she had been chosen with six other nurses to model clothes at a charity mannequin parade. The object of the show had been to raise funds for special equipment for the hospital and a famous dress designer had provided model frocks. Her father had attended and when he had seen her in this frock he had bought it for her, for a present. It was a creation of green and gold, cut and swathed with the utmost cunning, and showed Judy's perfect figure off to great advantage.

Judy put on her matching green pendant and earrings, a present from her mother, and stood back to get the full effect. She smiled, well pleased with her efforts; the Grecian style of the frock which left one arm and shoulder bare looked even more attractive now that she had acquired a light tan, and also her face was thinner than the last time she had worn the dress.

Mrs Palmer knocked on the door and came in. 'Oh, Judy, my dear, you look beautiful! What a dream of a dress. The children will be thrilled to see you.'

'Does Mark know I'm going out with Lucky?'

'No, I'm sure he doesn't. Lucky is ready whenever you are. He has an evening suit on and looks most dashing and distinguished. You look simply wonderful, I hope you have a very happy evening.' She kissed Judy lightly and walked to the door, then turned and looked at Judy again as she said, 'Mark is a stubborn fool, but I can't interfere.' She went out and closed the door.

Now the time had come to face Mark, Judy felt scared. Perhaps Lucky was right, perhaps she was a fool to go out with him. It was a ridiculous idea, she must have been crazy to think of it—still, she would have to go through with it now. She dabbed a little perfume on, then picked up her matching stole and went slowly along the passage to the kitchen. As she opened the door she heard Mark speaking.

'Well, apparently you've found yourself a partner for tonight, Lucky.'

Judy slipped into the room, 'Yes, Mark, he found me.' She looked at Mark, her eyes bright and challenging, her chin high. Mark just stared at her, while Lucky was on his feet in an instant. 'Exquisite, my dear, exquisite. That dress suits you to perfection.'

The twins hung back for a moment, then Vicki clapped her hands, 'Oh, isn't she gorgeous, Uncle Mark? Look, she's almost as pretty as Mummy.'

Mark spoke at last. 'Yes, Vicki, Judy is beautiful. I've told her so before. Do you remember, Judy?'

Judy remembered very well the night they had walked home from the orchard, and how he had looked at her that night. She felt the lump in her throat would choke her.

Mark continued as if her answer did not matter, 'Lucky, you can't take that vision out in your old van. Borrow my car for the night. It's at the front gate, the keys are in it.'

'Come with me, Judy,' Lucky said, offering his arm. 'We'll travel in style tonight. Thanks for the car, Mark. I really appreciate your offer. I'll take good care of it.'

'It's more important that you take good care of Judy,' Mark replied.

Judy's eyes were bright with unshed tears, as she walked down the path. The dress meant nothing at all. Mark did not care who she went out with. Lucky closed the door, then went round to the driver's seat. He started the car and moved off smoothly. 'Beautiful car, it was decent of Mark to lend it to us,' he commented.

'He didn't care, Lucky. I shouldn't have bothered you to take me out.'

'You think he didn't care? You're very much mistaken, my chicken. He was boiling mad at me. Now cheer up, you're going to enjoy yourself tonight, make no mistake about that. No girl goes out with me and sits weeping over another man; I wouldn't allow it.'

They had an excellent dinner at a hotel, then went to the cabaret. Perhaps it was because Judy had not been out since she arrived on the Coast, perhaps it was because she had Lucky for a partner, but whatever the reason the evening began to swing. It was one of those evenings when everything goes well, a night to remember for years. Judy loved dancing and Lucky was a superb partner, the music was wonderful. In between dances they talked and laughed, or were entertained by interesting and exciting floor shows.

The party they were with were all older than Judy, and they made much of her, the women were frankly envious of her dress and the men showered her with compliments. The drinks were cold, the music intoxicating and the conversation at the table was witty and sophisticated. Judy loved the laughter, the excitement and the gaiety, and her eyes sparkled with fun.

Some time after supper Lucky asked her if she was tired, and if she wanted to go home.

'No, not yet, I'm having a wonderful time. But of course, if you have had enough I don't mind leaving.'

'No, I don't want to go,' replied Lucky. 'I can't remember when I've enjoyed myself more. You certainly have a way of spreading joy around the place, but you make me realize my age. I think dancing round and round this room is harder than going up on the tops.'

'On the tops of what?' asked Judy.

'Up in the mountains, on top of the hills,' explained Lucky. 'Each month I get three or four days off because I work straight through Saturdays and Sundays, you see. Well, if the weather is good I get away up the bush and do a bit of shooting. I'll take you with me next time I go, it's a great feeling to get away up there, away from everyone, you come back refreshed and ready to take your place in this dingy old world with more tranquillity. How about it?'

'No, thanks, although I would love to go, I think I'd better stay on the flat and admire them from a distance.'

At last the band played 'Auld Lang Syne', the party broke up, and the couples left the hall.

Lucky asked as they drove away, 'Have you any idea what time it is?'

Judy giggled happily. 'Haven't a clue. Does it matter?'

'Four-thirty. We're going to get home with the milk.'

'Oh, milking! I forgot you'll have to get up for milking. You'll only get half an hour in bed.'

'It causes you some amusement? You think it funny?' Lucky growled.

'Hilariously funny,' laughed Judy, knowing she could go to bed and sleep as late as she wished.

As they walked through the gate and stopped by the back door the sky was turning pearly pink with the dawn. 'Thank you, Lucky, for the most wonderful evening. I loved every minute of it.'

'Did you think of Mark?'

'Not once.'

'Liar! I saw you looking dreamy-eyed during some of those oh-so-sad love songs—however, I'll forgive you. You don't think I'll let you off with a pretty thank-you, do you?'

Judy leaned up and gave him a kiss on the cheek, as light as a butterfly.

Lucky laughed, 'Go on, get to bed. I must be getting soft!'

It was after ten when Judy awoke. The children were at Sunday school, so she had tea and toast with Mrs Palmer and told her all the highlights of the evening.

'I'm glad you went out and had such a good time,' smiled Nan. 'Listening to you tell about the entertainment is nearly as good as being there to see it for myself.'

Judy wandered over to the shed to see

Lucky. As she walked under the louvre windows she heard her name mentioned so she stopped.

'You leave Judy alone, Lucky. She's not your type of girl.'

'Do tell?' Lucky's soft voice made Judy giggle, but she clapped her hand over her mouth quickly. She knew she shouldn't listen, but she could not resist.

'Yes, you keep away from her. I'm warning you, if she gets hurt through you I'll break every bone in your body. She's had a pretty rough time since she came to New Zealand and I don't want to see her get mixed up with you and your crowd. I don't see why you invited her out in the first place.'

'You'd be surprised if I told you why.' Judy held her breath. He wasn't going to tell!

There was a silence for a minute or two, then she heard Lucky again. 'What's it to you anyhow? You're a proper dog in the manger, Palmer—you don't want her yourself and you don't want to have anyone else to take her out and give her a good time. I think she's an attractive young lady, and I'll ask her out if I want to, so belt up.'

'You'll bring her nothing but trouble, Lucky. You're a married man, so leave her alone. I've got nothing against you personally except that your reputation with women stinks and Judy is a nice girl.'

'Have you never heard of divorce? What say have you got, anyhow? She's not your girl. I tried to give you the tickets yesterday.'

'She's living in my house and under my protection. Understand?'

'Protection?' Lucky roared with laughing. 'That girl needs protection like I need a hole in the head! She's quite capable of looking after herself, believe me.'

Judy decided it was time she moved unless she wanted to be caught. She returned to the house with a happy smile on her face, and a lilt in her walk. She knew she should be ashamed of herself, but all's fair in love and war, and she did love Mark. She loved him with her whole heart. Lucky? Judy gave a little pirouette. Lucky was a darling, she had been right to trust him.

After lunch, when Lucky was leaving, he asked Judy to walk out to his van with him. 'So, my young Judy, I think you may consider your campaign a success, because Mark had a go at me this morning. I'll give you a ring occasionally during the month to keep the kettle on the boil, so to speak, and when I come back next month we'll have another night out.'

Judy put an impulsive hand on his arm. 'I can't thank you enough, but I don't want to become a nuisance to you.'

'You're not a nuisance, chicken. I find I'm enjoying myself in a very novel way. Don't look now, but Mark is watching. Would you like me to seize you in a passionate embrace and give him a display of my magnificent technique?'

Judy laughed delightedly. 'No, thanks, you've done more than enough already.'

'Whew! I was scared you would say yes, and the way your Mark is scowling at me I think I would have been lucky to leave here alive!'

Judy waved goodbye and then sauntered by Mark on her way inside. As she passed he caught her wrist. 'Do you like playing with fire?'

Judy smiled sweetly, 'If you mean do I like Lucky, the answer is yes!'

At that moment the twins arrived home from Sunday school and further conversation was impossible.

Vicki ran up. 'You stayed in bed awfully late this morning, Judy. I wanted to hear all about the dance. Mummy used to tell me what people wore and what she had to eat. Will you tell me now? Nan wouldn't let me wake you up this morning.'

'Yes, I'll tell you everything. Come on in, so I can talk while I put lunch on.'

The next day Mark went up to the flax and forgot to take his lunch, so Judy carried it up to where he was working beside the deep black lagoon. As she stood watching him work she had a feeling he had left his lunch behind on purpose so that he would be able to talk to her without interruption. He had been very quiet and stiff since lunch time yesterday. As he tied off a bundle of flax with unnecessary force, he threw it aside and turned to Judy. 'Thank you for bringing my lunch. Put it down there. I want to talk to you.'

Judy put down the lunch carefully, surprised to find her hands were shaking. Perhaps this was going to be the moment she had waited for, perhaps Mark was going to tell her he loved her, but as she turned towards him she realized that there was no love in his eyes, only anger. Immediately her fighting spirit was aroused.

'Are you going out with Lucky again?' His voice was hard.

'I might,' replied Judy casually.

'You're not very particular, are you?' Mark glared at her.

'Oh, I wouldn't say that, but he did take me out, which is more than I can say for you. A girl likes to be told she's pretty and fun to be with. Makes her feel good.' Judy was being deliberately provocative.

'I suppose he kissed you last night.'

'Well, not last night, actually, it was this morning,' she said blandly.

'And you enjoyed that too?' demanded Mark savagely.

'Since you ask, yes, I did rather.'

'You don't care who you go out with—any man will do? You don't care who kisses you —any man will do, is that what you mean?'

'You're catching on fast.' Judy moved further along the lagoon edge. 'Enjoy your lunch, Mark. I'm going home.'

In two strides he caught her, and holding her in an inflexible grip he kissed her three or four times—ruthless, insulting kisses with no love or affection in them.

'If that's all you want, why didn't you say? I don't mind obliging you.'

Judy's face was white. 'You beast, I hate you!' Her green eyes were flashing fire. She rushed at him, catching him off balance, and pushed him backwards into the lagoon, then turned and ran for her life. She headed away from home and down towards the river.

Her tears blinded her and she did not see Mac on the river bank until he touched her arm. 'What's the matter, lassie? Has someone been hurt?'

'No—yes, I have. I hate Mark, I hate him, I hate him!' And she threw herself down on the grass and cried as if her heart would break.

Mac sat beside her and gently stroked her hair until she lay quiet. 'Poor wee lassie, tell me about your trouble.'

Judy sat up wiping her eyes. 'Mark kissed me,' she sniffed.

'Did he now?' asked Mac without a glimmer of a smile. 'But I thought you wanted him to kiss you?'

'No, not like that! Oh, Mac, he kissed me as if he hated me!'

'Now why would he do a thing like that?' Mac pretended to be puzzled.

'Because I went out with Lucky on Saturday night,' Judy explained.

'Oh, ho, ho, ho, ho, fancy that? You went out with Lucky and Mark is angry with you? That's very good, and I'm sure it was what you had in mind. You scheming little minx!'

'Ye-e-s,' Judy answered hesitantly.

'Well, what are you complaining about?'

Judy brightened up and gave a small giggle. 'I pushed Mark into the lagoon, and I'm scared to go home. He looked so mad I think he'll kill me.'

'He will no kill you,' Mac hastened to assure her, 'but he may beat you, which would be no more than you deserve. Come on home with me, now. There's no use me staying here any longer, you've scared away all the fish.'

'I can't go home, Mac. I can't face Mark,' said Judy, getting to her feet. 'I'll have to leave. I can't stay here now.'

'I didn't think you were a coward, lassie. I'm disappointed in you.'

'It's all right for you to talk, you're not living in his house. He thinks I'm cheap. I'm going to pack my case.'

'You will do no such thing. You will say you are sorry to Mark for trying to drown him, and you will stay here until March. You told me you'd given your word to do that.'

'I won't say I'm sorry!' cried Judy passionately. 'Why should I? He deserved to be pushed in.'

'Now, now, lassie, you must apologize. It's always easier for a woman to say she's sorry than for a man. You don't want to leave in anger and not see Mark again, do you?' He strode along briskly, letting Judy trail behind while she tried to decide what to do.

When they came across the small bridge over Koromiko Creek, Mark was unloading the flax. As he was in dry clothes Judy presumed he had been inside to change. He still seemed to be very angry. Mac waited for Judy to catch up. 'Don't let your pride get in the way, Judy,' he said softly, then as they came closer to Mark he pushed her forward. 'Judy has something to say to you, Mark. I'll be on my way,' and Mac walked off.

Judy stood irresolute, if she walked away now there would be no returning. What was stopping her? Pride? She was to blame for the situation, she faced that honestly. She had meant to upset Mark, and he couldn't be expected to react just as she wanted him to. Suddenly she wanted to see him smile more than anything in the world. A wave of love for him swept over her, leaving her weak and shaken. What was pride compared to being friends with him again?

She put out her hand in a pleading gesture. 'I'm sorry, Mark, please forgive me. I can't bear it if you're angry with me.' She looked at the ground, fighting the tears. 'I didn't mean what I said up at the lagoon, you know I'm not like that. I was only trying to hurt you.'

The silence was unbearable. Wasn't he ever going to speak? She felt his hands gently on her shoulders and then she was drawn into the wonderful comfort of his arms, and she knew what Nan had meant when she said that love was comfort, courage, and a sense of belonging.

Mark whispered against her hair, 'Judy love, you make me feel even more of a heel than I was feeling already. If I forgive you will you forgive me? Oh, God, Judy, don't cry. I can't stand it. We're friends again now, stop crying. First you push me in the water, and now you're soaking my shirt. Do you want to give me pneumonia?'

Judy buried her head in his shoulder. Just a few minutes more in his arms, and then she would go. She had her answer; if he loved her he would have said so. All he could offer was friendship, and she would always treasure even that much of him.

'Please, Mark,' her voice was muffled. 'I

want you to release me from my promise to stay here till March. I want to go away. Zelda will be home next week, your mother told me. She can come and stay and look after your mother and the twins. Will you let me go?'

'No, you promised to stay no matter what happened, remember?'

Judy pushed herself away from him. 'Why wait until March to marry her? You could get married straight away and then I could leave. Please, Mark,' Judy pleaded. 'I've just got to go.'

'Yes, I'd look fine asking any girl to marry me now, wouldn't I, Judy? What would I say? Darling, would you marry me? I can't offer you much except love. I have a farm which I may lose before the end of the month, I have a mother to support, and if Paul and Betsy don't turn up I'll have a set of twins to bring up as well. If I lose the farm and go back to my job you'll get damn all to live on. Do you think any girl in her right mind would say yes to a proposal like that one, Judy?'

'If she loved you she would jump at the chance.' Judy's voice was low.

'Well, she isn't getting the chance.' Mark's voice was strained. 'I may be an optimistic fool to think I can swing this farm, but I'd be crazy to contemplate marriage with all the rest hanging over my head. Now go and make me a cup of tea, and if you ever shove me in the lagoon again I'll put you over my knee and paddle your bottom. Now get going!'

CHAPTER VIII

The next week was one of the happiest Judy had ever spent. She went fishing with Mac and Peter and earned their praise by catching a three-pound trout.

Peter was so proud of her, his very own pupil, and was not a bit deterred when Mac warned him that he would end up in gaol with Judy for encouraging her to fish without a licence.

'If the ranger came along, I'd take back the rod,' he explained happily. ''Course, Judy is so pretty she would only have to smile at him and he'd let her go.'

On Sunday Mark took them all out to a speedboat regatta at Lake Moana, and friends there gave Judy the thrill of her life by letting her try water-skiing. She spent more time in the water than on it, but it did not weaken her enthusiasm for the sport.

On the following Wednesday afternoon she came home to find Nan entertaining a visitor. Judy knew before Nan introduced them that this was Zelda. Judy had been prepared to hate her on sight, but before she had been in her company very long she knew she could not hate her. Zelda was small and slender, a quiet, shy girl with a very sweet smile. No wonder Mark felt protective towards her; any man would. Zelda spent a lot of time at the farm. She followed Mark around and Judy saw them having long earnest conversations.

Judy was jealous, horribly jealous. She could not bear the bitter heartache that came when she saw Mark put a carelessly casual arm around Zelda, or took her hand walking down the path. Judy despised herself for being resentful. She liked Zelda; she loved Mark; if she was a decent person she should have been pleased to see them so happy.

One night as she leaned out of her window gazing at the stars she saw them walk out to Zelda's car, Zelda's voice carried clearly to her. 'Oh, Mark, you are a silly fool! Money is nothing. You've got your values mixed, it's love that makes the world go round.'

Judy did not hear Mark's reply, but she did see him put his hands on Zelda's slight shoulders, just as he had done to her only a week ago. Judy turned away from the window. It was no use tormenting herself. Mark was her friend, but he loved Zelda. Three weeks more and she would be able to leave. Tomorrow she would go into town and buy her ticket. That would help her to accept the reality of her eventual, but definite, departure. She lay in bed, but did not sleep, nor did she cry. The pain she felt was too deep for tears; it was a tearing, aching loneliness for Mark's arms to be around her, for his lips to be on hers.

As she drove from Greymouth the next day she could see the huge mountain range, the Southern Alps, stretched out before her, in the distance. Strange how they had fascinated her from the day she had come to the farm. Suddenly she decided that before she left New Zealand she was going to take a trip to the mountains.

She remembered Lucky offering to take her that night at the cabaret. Of course she knew that he had been joking, and she had laughed at his offer, but she wasn't laughing now. Her determination strengthened as she drew nearer the farm. She would go. Mark did not care where she went or who she went with now; he had Zelda home.

The next time Lucky rang her she asked him when he was going on the tops again.

'It all depends on the weather, Judy. I have three days off next week, starting Wednesday. Why do you ask?'

'You offered to take me with you once. Well, now I want to go.'

'You've got to be joking!'

'No, I'm quite serious,' Judy assured him. 'I'm leaving for England on the first of March, and it's something I want to do before I leave. Will you take me, Lucky?'

'Like that, is it, chicken? Well, you can't win them all. I'm sorry.'

'Will you take me?' Judy pleaded.

'Sure, I'll take you. Let me think a minute. I know just the place for you. It's a stiffish climb, but you should manage it okay. Are you sure you want to go? Mark may not let you.'

'Mark won't be worried. He's otherwise occupied at the moment. What do I have to wear?'

'A comfortable pair of boots or shoes for a start, shorts and shirt if you want to, but bring a pair of slacks and a warm jersey in case it turns cold. We can go up and back in the one day, if we get an early start.'

'What's the name of the mountain I'm going to climb?'

'Round Hill.'

'I don't want a hill, I want to climb a mountain,' Judy argued.

'It's quite a hill. You'll do very well if you get to the top of it. It's about four thousand feet or a bit over. Do you want me to pick out a bigger one?' laughed Lucky.

'No, Round Hill will do nicely, thanks.' Then she had second thoughts. 'I've never done any climbing, Lucky. I don't know anything about ropes and all those fancy things you've got to do on rocks. Perhaps I might cause you too much trouble.'

'Oh, there's no need for roping, you'll do fine. It will be tough going for you, though, but let me warn you that once you start I won't let you turn back even if I have to drag you to the top by your hair. Still game to give it a go?'

'Yes.'

'Right, I'll give you a ring Tuesday night, just in case you change your mind. We'll have to start from here at four-thirty in the morning. See you!' and he hung up.

Judy listened anxiously to the weather report and was reassured to hear 'fine weather' predicted. On Tuesday night after Lucky rang Judy returned to the dinner table.

'May I have the day off tomorrow, please, Mark?'

Mark looked surprised. 'Why, sure. Going somewhere?'

'I'm going away for the whole day. I'll be leaving at four-thirty a.m., and I won't be back until quite late. You don't mind, do you, Nan?'

'Not at all, dear. Don't worry about me, I'm disgustingly healthy these days.'

Judy knew this was far from the truth, because as day followed day, and no news came from South America, Nan seemed to grow more frail. Judy worried about her, but there was nothing she could do except insist on making her rest each afternoon.

'Where are you going, Judy?' asked Vicki.

'I bet I know,' Peter said. 'Someone is taking you to Christchurch and back. Am I right?'

'No, guess again.'

'I know, I know!' shouted Vicki. 'You're going to the glaciers?'

'Wrong again,' teased Judy. 'You'd never guess in a hundred years.'

'The Pancake Rocks?—no, you wouldn't have to start that early,' Peter guessed again. 'The glow-worm caves and the greenstone factory at Hokitika?' When Judy shook her head Vicki urged, 'Tell us, Judy, where are you going?'

'I'm going to climb a mountain.'

Peter questioned, 'Which one? How high is it? Who's taking you?'

Judy smiled, 'Well, it's not really a mountain. The name is Round Hill and it's over four thousand feet high, and I'm going right to the very top.'

'Have you had any climbing experience, Judy?' Mark's tone was cautious.

'None at all, but I'll have an expert guide,' Judy answered pleasantly.

'Lucky?' Mark spat the name out.

'Yes, Lucky.' Judy's own temper started to rise. He was not going to stop her.

'You're very foolish. I warned you not to go out with him. I thought you had more sense.'

'Don't you think Lucky is a competent guide?' Judy asked innocently.

'Oh, he's good all right, one of the best— half mountain goat, but that isn't what I meant, as you very well know.'

'Oh, you're still banging on about his reputation. I've booked my ticket on the plane and I'm leaving in ten days' time. I want to go up to the mountains before I leave. In fact, I want to enjoy as many new experiences as I can before I go.' Her green eyes challenged him.

'I forbid you to go!' Mark shouted.

Judy pushed her chair away from the table. 'You can't stop me. You've got no right to try. You look after Zelda, I'll look after myself.' She turned and ran from the room, out of the gate and up on to the bridge. Leaning on the rail, she looked down into the swift-moving water. Why did she have to lose her temper and make a mess of everything? She had intended to be calm and collected even if Mark tried to stop her, but she had shouted back at him, like a virago. She was bitterly ashamed of herself. Only a few weeks ago she had been so happy and content to be his friend, but that had been before Zelda had returned. Since then she had tried to control her feelings, but tonight, in one flash of temper she had spoiled her hopes of being able to leave here pretending she did not care. Mark, oh, Mark! She loved him so much she would have died for him. But she wouldn't die, she thought drearily. She would go on living. Back in England the days would pass and the pain would gradually grow less. Some day she would be able to look back on her visit to New Zealand as a wonderful memory. Nursing would fill her life, she would make it do so. She returned to the house in a more reasonable frame of mind.

Nan had started the dinner dishes, so Judy picked up a tea towel. 'I'm so sorry, Nan. I hope I didn't upset you, but Mark had no business trying to stop me from going with Lucky.'

'I'm not upset, Judy dear. You have a perfect right to go where you like, but do be careful.'

'Be careful of Lucky or of the mountain, Nan?'

'Both,' answered Nan with a wicked smile. 'He's a most attractive man.'

'I'm in no danger from Lucky's charms. He doesn't interest me, except as a friend, but as I'm leaving, I would like to do this trip. The mountains have fascinated me ever since I came here. I have a feeling that when I get to the top of my mountain, my troubles will look very small and insignificant.'

'I understand, Judy.' Nan's voice was kind.

They finished the dishes in silence, both busy with their own thoughts. As Judy hung up the tea towel she asked, 'Where are the twins? Have they gone to bed?'

'No, they went to see Mac. Oh, Judy, I am upset over you leaving. I never interfere with my children's lives, but this time I've been sorely tempted. I had hoped that you and Mark...' She sighed deeply.

'Don't, Nan!' Judy's voice was sharp. Then she took a deep breath. 'I love Mark, I suppose you've guessed that, but he loves Zelda, so I must leave. I thought I'd like to tell you. It's nice to know that you would have welcomed me, but don't let us talk about it any more, please.'

'The twins were worried about your leaving. That's why they went over to see Mac; they head for him when they feel Mark and I are not coping with their problems in a satisfactory manner. They're going to miss you terribly, and so am I. You must write to me when you leave here, I'll remember your kindness always; you've become like one of the family, and I hate to see you go.'

Judy's eyes were bright with tears. 'I've loved it here...' her voice shook. 'I must be tired. If you don't mind I'll go to bed, I have to get up so early in the morning.' She kissed Mrs Palmer and went through to her room. Only ten more days to go. Could she stand ten more days of this stupid, self-inflicted torture? Of hoping for the impossible? Hoping that perhaps at the last minute Mark might find out that he loved her, and not Zelda? It was a good thing that she would be away tomorrow, even one day in the mountains might give her the tranquillity that Lucky spoke of. She certainly needed something to carry her through these next few days.

Judy set the alarm for four o'clock. That would give her time to have something to eat before Lucky came.

When the alarm shrilled she quickly switched it off, jumped out of bed and washed and dressed. She wore her slacks over her shorts because it was still fairly cold. She could take them off later if she felt too hot. A feeling of exhilaration took hold of her. Today she was going to climb her mountain. She picked up her thick jersey and hurried out to the kitchen, then stopped dead at the sight of Mark by the stove.

'Come on, sit down—one breakfast coming up.' He spoke quite cheerfully. 'It's a long drive out to the Kopara. You'll travel all the better for eating a good meal before you start.'

Judy felt rather bewildered. 'Why, thanks, Mark. You shouldn't have bothered. I could have got something for myself. You're not trying to stop me, then?'

The smile he gave her was warm and friendly. 'No, I was stupid, not you. I'm very glad you're having this trip. Lucky is a good chap in the hills, but you must be careful. Take it easy for a start, and take a rest when you need it. Don't let Lucky hurry you too much. I've done that climb many times. If I had known that you wanted to go I would have taken you myself.'

Judy felt a pang of regret. It would have been marvellous to go there with Mark; then she remembered how he could not take a day off work for any relaxation. 'Yes, it would have been nice to go with you, Mark, but you're always so busy. You couldn't spare the time. You have to use every minute trying to save your farm.'

Mark had a peculiar expression on his face. 'It isn't the farm that has come between us, Judy. I would chuck the farm tomorrow...' he stopped suddenly. 'Forget it, nothing has changed. Drink up your tea, I can hear Lucky's van coming down the hill.'

Just as they were going out the door, the phone shrilled and Mark said, 'Damn, I'll have to answer it, or it will wake the whole household. Have a good day.'

Judy walked slowly out to the truck. For a moment back there in the kitchen, for one whole heart-stopping, breathless moment, she had thought her dreams were coming true, but of course that was impossible. She had too much imagination, that was the trouble. She kept trying to read hidden meanings into Mark's words and glances, and there was nothing there at all. Snap out of it, Judy, she told herself, this is your day to climb to the sky, to pack up your troubles and throw them to the winds. She greeted Lucky with a gay smile. 'Hullo, I'm ready. Let's get going.'

'Good girl! You know, I could get attached to you, you never keep me waiting,' remarked Lucky as they drove off. 'It will take us about an hour to the old Mill, and then you're for it. It takes me about an hour and a half by myself to climb to the top, but dragging you with me, we should take an hour longer, maybe more. I'd like to get a shot if I can, might get some good velvet.'

'What do you mean, velvet?' queried Judy.

'Each year the stags shed their antlers and grow new ones. While they're soft and new they feel like velvet to touch, so the stags are said to be in the velvet. Later the antlers harden in time for the mating season, that's when the stags roar for their mates, and they need their antlers nice and sharp to fight their rivals off.'

'But what do you want the velvet for?'

'Money. They pay big money for a good set of velvet. It's exported to China, I believe they grind it up and use it for medicinal purposes, but I don't much care, just as long as they keep paying out fantastic prices for it.'

'Why don't you settle down, Lucky? Don't you get sick of being in a different house every night?'

'Now, Judy, we'll remain friends on one condition, and that is you must not try and reform me. How did we get on to this subject, anyhow? My mother is always telling me a rolling stone gathers no moss, and who wants to gather moss? Not me, I can assure you.'

'I was wondering, that's all. However, if it worries you, I can promise you I won't try and reform you. For one thing, I have only nine days left, and I'm sure reforming you would take me much longer.'

'True,' answered Lucky with a grin. After they had driven about twenty miles, he said, 'In a few minutes I'm going to show you something special.'

'What is it?'

'Wait and see.' They were driving along a narrow, gravel road, which spiralled down a steep hill, the bush so close on either side that the tall trees sometimes met overhead, making an archway of green. Lucky stopped the car. 'Well, what do you think of that view?'

Judy looked out at a beautiful lake, which was as smooth and still as a mirror, reflecting the snow-capped mountains in all their glory.

'Oh, what a wonderful sight!'

'Not too bad,' replied Lucky as they drove on. 'Won't be long now. In about ten minutes I'll be able to show you Round Hill. We'll stop on the Bluff and you can see it clearly, then I'll take you up for a closer inspection.'

When he stopped, he pointed. 'See, over there—no, not the high craggy one with the snow on, the one to the left, that's Round Hill.

The big one is Mount Elizabeth. You would need a bit of training before you could tackle that one.' He let the clutch out gently and the car moved on down the hill. They drove about three miles up a farm road and stopped by an old abandoned sawmill.

'From here on it's Shanks' Pony,' said Lucky. 'The old van wouldn't make it far in the bush.'

Judy noticed how much more natural and relaxed Lucky had become as they came nearer to the bush. He had lost that bored cynical expression he usually wore.

They set sail, Lucky leading and carrying the pack, Judy behind with the rifle. The first quarter of an hour was easy, a gradual climb along an overgrown disused road, which, although little more than two ruts up the ridge, at least gave good footing and free passage for their taut, straining bodies. The second growth and rushes underfoot were still wet with the heavy overnight dew. The road petered out into a creek-bed, wide at this point and scoured with past flooding, caused by the torrential rains which fell frequently and without warning in these mountains, Lucky explained to her.

They followed up the creek, gaining altitude until the gully began to close in and there was only just room for Lucky to squeeze through with the encumbrance of his pack. When a narrow side stream came tumbling in on his left Lucky turned towards the opposite face and started to climb.

'Give me the rifle, Judy, and take a breather.'

Judy's legs were trembling and her mouth was parched and dry; she was only too pleased to hand over the rifle which had seemed so light when they started and now weighed a ton, by the feel of it.

She climbed after Lucky, following in his footsteps, grasping the trees he grasped, and being determined not to be left behind. After fifteen minutes of almost vertical climb they came out on to a ridge and the going became easier. Below them she could still hear the creek bubbling and gurgling its way down to the river, although the sight of it was denied her by the steepness of the face they had just climbed. On either side the ridge fell steeply away to disappear into an impenetrable wall of green forest.

Above them a brief glimpse of the sunlight could be seen, through a gap in the green canopy caused by the falling of a huge rimu tree. Lucky told Judy that these trees lived to be over one thousand years old, and she wondered what sort of life people lived in New Zealand when it had been a seedling the size of the one beside her. It was at least fifty feet tall, reaching for the sunlight, dead straight and no thicker than her wrist. Then she chided herself, there were probably no people living here then—after all, New Zealand was only discovered by Abel Tasman in 1642, and the Maoris had migrated here about A.D. 1350. At least she had learned that much by helping the twins with their homework.

'We mustn't stop for more than a couple of minutes,' said Lucky, 'or your muscles will stiffen up on you. Got to keep a sweat up. Come on!'

'Ladies don't sweat, they perspire,' argued Judy as she scrambled to her feet.

'Same difference,' remarked Lucky. 'And you don't fool me, you're just trying to start an argument so that you can get a longer spell.'

Ahead of them the ridge rose steadily and the footing was much better. They were walking on a carpet of leaves and moss; there was silence except for the harshness of their breathing. Twenty minutes after their brief rest by the creek bed Lucky pointed out to Judy that they were leaving the rimu trees behind and that the birch trees were becoming smaller, and their branches nearer the ground.

When she asked about a big tree beside the track Lucky answered, 'That's a rata. You can pick them out easily from the flat when they're in flower. They have a brilliant scarlet flower. Ten years ago this hill used to be a mass of scarlet blooms in January, but a blight got the trees and now only the odd one flowers. Some people say that the opossums killed the trees, but it's not so. Most of the opossums hang round the edges of the bush and eat the farmers' turnips and grass.'

An hour and a half away from the van, after taking a two-minute rest every twenty minutes, Judy thought she must be going delirious with fatigue, because she suddenly smelt her favourite fruit—bananas.

She stopped, wiped the perspiration out of her eyes and looked around. She noticed that they had left all the big trees behind, the ridge had broadened out and she could see for several hundred yards. Beside her grew a tree about twenty feet high from which came the delicious banana smell.

'Banana tree,' replied Lucky in answer to her query. 'Don't get excited, though, they don't have any fruit on them. They look like the real thing with their broad leaves, don't they? The smell comes from the bark which they shed every year. It's saved plenty of blokes who've been bushed overnight, because the bark and limbs will burn easily even when they're wet. We're getting well up the mountain now, because they only grow around the three thousand to three thousand five hundred feet mark.'

Judy found everything Lucky had to say of absorbing interest. He was a wonderful guide, but she did not see how he had the breath to talk, when she needed every ounce of strength just to keep walking.

'Same as this stuff,' continued Lucky, pointing to a scrub about a foot high. 'Monkey scrub. It's a fair cow if you get off the track. This stuff grows very thick around three thousand five hundred feet up and the snow gets on it and crushes it down. It doesn't die, just spreads out and grows up again all round. It's sometimes so thick and matted that you have to go over the top of it like a monkey would. Hurry up, we'll be out in the open in about twenty minutes.'

Gradually the scrub became more sparse and the mountain top came into view. The track was not so steep now and almost disappeared among the flax bushes, which were no more than three feet high. Then they came to a small waterhole set in a tiny flat at the foot of a ridge, the junction of two gullies. The flax here was taller and the banana trees and monkey scrub afforded them some protection from the keen early morning breeze, still chilled by the light dew.

'Let's have a brew-up,' Lucky said. 'There's still a lot of mist on the tops, and we'll have to wait for it to lift if we want to get a good shot.'

Judy sagged to the ground and was content to watch Lucky busy himself preparing a fire and filling a billy. 'How far to the top?' she asked.

178

'It will take us about half an hour or a bit more, but there's quite a good view from here. Have a look when you've recovered.'

Immediately below them they could see the lake still covered here and there with wisps of early morning mist. From the lake shore the bush ran away into ridges and gullies rounded off and softened by the trees' leafy camouflage. Green gave way to white as the snow caps of the main divide followed through to Mount Cook, the monarch of them all, looming high even at a hundred miles away.

Lucky showed her on the right where the green gave way to blue, the deep blue of midnight, the turbulent Tasman Sea. Through the hills he plotted the course of the Grey River wandering on its way to the Tasman. Pockets of mist clung here and there in the valleys. Where the Grey River finished, its joining at Greymouth could be pinpointed by the tinge of red from the red-painted roofs.

'It's about thirty miles to Greymouth, as the crow flies,' remarked Lucky. 'Come on, finish your tea and we'll get on to the top.'

'That was a great cup of tea, Lucky. It's given me enough strength to make it to the top, I hope. Nice to find a waterhole handy, just when I was about to die of exhaustion!'

'Tarn, Judy, not waterhole.' He pulled her

to her feet, 'Walk, or I'll drag you, cave man style!'

Judy forced her aching limbs to carry her up the last ridge, and finally she made the summit. What a grand sense of achievement she felt.

'Well now, I'm going to cross over to the second peak. Do you want to come with me or do you want to stay here? There's nothing on these hills to hurt you. It's ten o'clock; it will take me a couple of hours to go over and back.'

'I'll stay here,' said Judy. 'This is the nearest I've ever been to heaven. I could sit and look at this view for hours. Why didn't you tell me to bring a camera?'

Lucky raised an eyebrow. 'Do you think you could have made it carrying a camera?' he laughed. 'You did jolly well, I shouldn't tease you. You were much better than I thought possible. Well, I'm off. You're as safe as a church here provided you don't wander off. Move down by that tarn if you feel cold. We'll have venison for lunch.' He moved off with the easy tireless tread of an experienced mountaineer.

Judy lay back in the tussocks and gazed at the blue sky, with the little white clouds scuttling across it. This was her mountain. With Lucky gone she had it all to herself, she was completely alone and filled with a strange sense of peace, and something more, a touch of excitement and expectancy. This was her mountain and somehow, some time before she went down it was going to give her the courage she needed to smile when Mark and Zelda announced their plans. Something would be given to her to help her hold her head high for the next nine days. She wasn't in a hurry, she just relaxed and waited. Slowly her eyes closed and she fell asleep.

When she awoke the sun was high overhead. Lucky would be back soon. She went down to the tarn and washed her face and hands in the cool clear water. She watched the water settle and become smooth, then looked at her reflection in the water. She stiffened and stared. The water reflected the figure of a man standing behind her, and it wasn't Lucky. Nervously she turned.

'Mark!' she said incredulously. She could hardly believe her eyes. She put her hand out and touched him, just in case she was dreaming.

'Oh, I'm real enough,' Mark said, smiling that wicked teasing smile that she loved so much.

'What are you doing here?' Judy could not accept the fact that he was on the mountain side with her.

'I came up here to ask you to marry me.'

Judy shut her eyes. It must be a mirage. She had never heard of people seeing a mirage in the mountains, but this sudden vision of

Mark could not be real.

She felt his arms enfold her and draw her close. 'Will you marry me, Judy, love? I love you so much, I can't let you go. I won't ever let you go. Say yes, my darling.'

For an answer she opened her eyes and put her arms around his neck, drawing his lips down to hers.

A long time later he asked, 'Where's Lucky?'

'He went across to the second peak shooting. He should be back soon.'

Mark held her tight, 'Oh, Judy, how I've longed to take you in my arms and call you my own. You have no idea the control I've had to keep on myself to stop me from doing so, and damning the consequences.'

'But why, Mark, why didn't you tell me?'

'When you left this morning as the phone was ringing, I was feeling quite desperate. I thought I'd lost you for ever, and I cursed the phone. But when I answered it, it was the exchange to say that there was a call coming through from South America and to wait around for it. I had to wait over an hour before the call came through, and it was Paul, to tell that he and Betsy were safe and returning to New Zealand by plane next week.'

'How wonderful!' Judy's eyes shone. 'Oh, dear Nan will be so relieved. At last her faith has been rewarded.'

'Yes, it's great news, in more ways than one. It meant that I could ask you to marry me. I nearly started off after you there and then, but first I had to wake Nan and tell her. She was rather overcome, so I made her stay in bed. When I told the twins their mother and father would be home next week they went completely crazy, like a pair of lunatics, so it took me ages to get their lunches ready and feed them breakfast. I thought they were better at school, it would help them to settle down. By the time I got them on the bus I was hours late with the milking, and the more I hurried to get to you the more things went wrong.' He pulled her close and kissed her.

As Judy drew away she asked, 'But why did you have to wait to hear from Paul before you could ask me to marry you? You would have saved us both so much pain and heartache. You knew I loved the twins, and had their parents not come back, I would have loved to help you with them. Didn't you trust me that far?' Her voice was sad.

'Of course I trusted you, darling, and loved you. I loved you from the moment I found you, oh, so beautiful, and oh, so angry, in my car. But how could I ask you to marry me? There was not only the twins, but Nan only has her pension. She was also my responsibility, and would have had to live with us.'

'As if that would have worried me!' Judy interrupted indignantly.

'I know, I know, but there was always the chance I would lose the farm. If I could have counted on swinging the farm I would have risked it, but it's always been so close to the margin I couldn't be sure. If I lost that and had to take another farm advisory appointment, my salary wouldn't have stretched to you, as well as Nan and the twins.'

'And now it can.' Judy nestled closer to him.

'Yes, now Paul and Betsy will come home and take their horrible little brats away, and Nan will live with them as she has always done. You and I will be together, perhaps not on the farm, but I don't care, just as long as we're together.'

A thought struck Judy. 'What about Zelda? Is she going to be terribly hurt?'

'She is not, you silly goose. Zelda has been a good friend to me, and always will be, but nothing more. She's keen on a chap she met in Aussie. She's been giving me the works because I wasn't honest with you, but I felt it was better, if you had to go, not to complicate matters further by telling you I loved you but had no hope of being able to marry you.'

'Okay, okay, break it up!' Lucky was back. 'You'd think when a bloke brings a girl four thousand feet up a mountain that he could at least be sure of being safe leaving her alone for a couple of hours. I came back an hour ago, but saw you were busy, so I roamed around being tactful, but enough is enough. I'm starving. We're having venison for lunch —that is, if food isn't too mundane a subject to mention.'

Mark built the fire while Lucky prepared the venison. Judy thought the meal was delicious; she was really hungry after the climb and even being in love had not affected her appetite.

As they tidied up Lucky remarked, 'I suppose congratulations are in order. You want to watch her, Mark, she's too fond of getting her own way. Don't ever let her get the upper hand or you're done for!'

'I'll keep your advice in mind, Lucky,' Mark replied with a grin.

'Well, seeing you're here, you can have the responsibility of taking her home. I'll stay up here the night and have another go tomorrow, if that's okay by you.'

'Thank you for bringing me, Lucky. It has been a marvellous trip,' said Judy as she watched Lucky pack his gear into the pack.

'Right, that's settled,' Lucky said as he straightened up, and looked at Mark. 'As I won't be at your wedding, do you mind if I kiss the bride now? I've danced miles round the ballroom with her, dragged her miles up this damned hill without getting a kiss, and I reckon I deserve one. So with your permission . . . ?'

To Judy's surprise, Mark nodded, and Lucky took her in his arms and kissed her with practised skill. 'If he doesn't treat you right, chicken, you just let me know.' He picked up his pack and gave them a mock salute. 'So long, mates, see you around.'

Judy watched him striding away, and thought what a good friend he had been to her, and just now his words and action had been to clear any small doubts that Mark might have been harbouring in his mind concerning their friendship. Lucky reached the ridge, turned and waved and disappeared from view.

Judy and Mark did not hurry home. Their love was so precious, so new, they wished to keep their wonderful experience to themselves, if only for a few hours.

The wedding was over, and Judy sat by Mark as he drove the car through the traffic. On her finger was a square-cut emerald ring and a wide band of bright gold, her wedding ring. Mac had provided the gold for her ring, and offered it with his customary dignity, wishing them lifelong happiness. A tender smile touched Judy's lips as she thought of Nan's loving kindness and Vicki's wild excitement when she and Mark had returned from the hill. Peter had been quite smug, pointing out that he had suggested Mark should marry Judy ages ago. Paul and Betsy had arrived home and then the wedding had been arranged. Zelda had been delighted when Judy had asked her to be bridesmaid, and Vicki had been a beautiful flower-girl. Judy turned to smile at Mark, her husband, all the love in her heart shining in her eyes.

Mark pulled over on to a quiet part of the road. 'Don't you dare look at me like that when I'm driving, my lovely, lovely wife, or you may have us off the road!' He took her in his arms and kissed her.

Later he said, 'You know, I'm a remarkably lucky fellow. Today I got myself a wife. She may not be much to look at, but she can cook, and a man can't have everything. Now, now control that nasty temper!' He kissed her again, then continued. 'I haven't had time to tell you, but I also own a farm. Yes, old James, the solicitor, gave me the title deeds at the wedding—a present from Uncle Jack, the old rascal. He apparently wanted me to have the farm all the time, but he also wanted to make me sweat a bit first. The clause about me marrying Zelda was only to make sure I *didn't* marry her. He told old James that she wasn't the girl for me, and he knew me well enough to know that if he put that clause in the will, Zelda would be the last girl I would marry. Cunning old devil! I wish he could have seen the beauty I picked for myself.'

' 'Oh, Mark,' whispered Judy as he drew her close, 'I love you so much . . .' and that was all she had time to say.

GOLDEN HARLEQUIN LIBRARY

Now 24 Volumes!

Harlequin readers will be delighted! We've collected seventy two of your all-time favourite Harlequin Romance novels to present to you in an attractive new way. It's the Golden Harlequin Library.

Each volume contains three complete, unabridged Harlequin Romance novels, most of which have not been available since the original printing. Each volume is exquisitely bound in a fine quality rich gold hardcover with royal blue imprint. And each volume is priced at an unbelievable $1.75. That's right! Handsome, hardcover library editions at the price of paperbacks!

This very special collection of 24 volumes (there'll be more!) of classic Harlequin Romances would be a distinctive addition to your library. And imagine what a delightful gift they'd make for any Harlequin reader!

Start your collection now. See reverse of this page for full details.

GOLDEN HARLEQUIN LIBRARY — $1.75 each volume

FREE!

Have You Missed Any of These Harlequin Romances?

☐ 1009 NURSE AT FAIRCHILDS
　　　Marjorie Norrell
☐ 1011 THE TURQUOISE SEA
　　　Hilary Wilde
☐ 1013 MARY INTO MAIR
　　　Jane Ray
☐ 1017 ATTACHED TO DOCTOR
　　　MARCHMONT　　Juliet Shore
☐ 1021 FOLLY TO BE WISE
　　　Sara Seale
☐ 1024 THE HOUSE OF DISCONTENT
　　　Esther Wyndham
☐ 1027 THE LONELY SHORE
　　　Anne Weale
☐ 1030 THE BLACK BENEDICTS
　　　Anita Charles
☐ 1076 BELLS IN THE WIND
　　　Kate Starr
☐ 1100 THE BROKEN WING
　　　Mary Burchell
☐ 1108 SUMMER EVERY DAY
　　　Jane Arbor
☐ 1145 YOUNG DOCTOR YERDLEY
　　　Anne Durham
☐ 1173 RED AS A ROSE
　　　Hilary Wilde
☐ 1184 THE HOUSE OF OLIVER
　　　Jean S. Macleod
☐ 1199 JOHNNY NEXT DOOR
　　　Margaret Malcolm
☐ 1227 A MAN APART
　　　Jane Donnelly
☐ 1231 IMITATION MARRIAGE
　　　Phyllis Matthewman
☐ 1234 DESERT GOLD
　　　Pamela Kent
☐ 1249 DOCTOR ARNOLD'S AMBITION
　　　Pauline Ash
☐ 1254 THE MASTER OF KEILLS
　　　Jean S Macleod
☐ 1257 DOCTOR AT VILLA RONDA
　　　Iris Danbury
☐ 1270 THOUGH WORLDS APART
　　　Mary Burchell
☐ 1277 STRANGER'S TRESPASS
　　　Jane Arbor
☐ 1280 THE FLIGHT OF THE SWAN
　　　Eleanor Farnes
☑ 1290 A SUMMER TO LOVE
　　　Roumelia Lane

☐ 1291 MASTER OF GLENKEITH
　　　Jean S. Macleod
☐ 1294 THE BREADTH OF HEAVEN
　　　Rosemary Pollock
☐ 1296 THE WIND AND THE SPRAY
　　　Joyce Dingwell
☐ 1299 THE LISTENING PALMS
　　　Juliet Shore
☐ 1303 STILL WATERS
　　　Marguerite Lees
☐ 1305 DOCTOR GEYER'S PROJECT
　　　Marjorie Norrell
☐ 1306 A HANDFUL OF SILVER
　　　Isobel Chace
☐ 1310 TAWNY ARE THE LEAVES
　　　Wynne May
☐ 1315 WHERE THE KOWHAI BLOOMS
　　　Mary Moore
☐ 1320 SPANISH LACE
　　　Joyce Dingwell
☐ 1325 NO SOONER LOVED
　　　Pauline Garner
☐ 1331 HOTEL BELVEDERE
　　　Iris Danbury
☐ 1337 THE CAMPBELLS ARE COMING
　　　Felicity Hayle
☐ 1344 THE DANGEROUS DELIGHT
　　　Violet Winspear
☐ 1352 THE MOUNTAIN OF STARS
　　　Catherine Airlie
☐ 1357 RIPPLES IN THE LAKE
　　　Mary Coates
☐ 1361 SISTER PETERS IN
　　　AMSTERDAM　　Betty Neels
☐ 1367 INTERLUDE IN ARCADY
　　　Margery Hilton
☐ 1370 THE WAYS OF LOVE
　　　Catherine Airlie
☐ 1374 FORTUNE'S LEAD
　　　Barbara Perkins
☐ 1380 RELUCTANT MASQUERADE
　　　Henrietta Reid
☐ 1389 MAN OF THE FOREST
　　　Hilda Pressley
☐ 1396 BRIGHT WILDERNESS
　　　Gwen Westwood
☐ 1400 THE DISTANT TRAP
　　　Gloria Bevan
☐ 1404 DIAMONDS ON THE LAKE
　　　Mary Cummins

All books are 50c.　Please use the handy order coupon.